The Clock That Stopped Time

A Story Inspired by Real Dreams of A Crystal Clock that Could Stop and Alter time.

G.J. Sarson

- ISBN-13 : 979-8301473920

Genre: Mythical Fiction, Fantasy, Adventure

The story is inspired by a variety of moments and dreams in real life. It is a Mythical Fictional Story of Crystal Powers and the Origin of Time.

For Lena, the dreams were recurring dreams of a crystal clock that could stop time. Lena was seemingly always late in getting assignments in for school. In Grade 6, my Social Studies Teacher gave an assignment to the class to write a short story on anything. Lena did not complete mine on time and when Lena was asked to read mine in front of the class, she had to admit it wasn't complete. Her mother was notified and that evening she sat with my mother and wrote out a story from my dreams about a crystal clock that stopped time. It wasn't a traditional clock. It was a giant crystal in the center of a crystal cave. In her dreams, sometimes she would touch the surface of the crystal and time would stop. It allowed her to go anywhere and only she was moving.

The next day at the beginning of class Lena was asked to read her story. As she read it, she could see her class mates were interested, but her stern teacher grabbed the half read story out of her hands, slapped her face and made kneel on her desk in front of the class for lying about creating the story. This incident made withdraw from those around her. But the dreams continued and Lena kept quiet. The dreams continued and became a passion of hers to try and understand what the meaning of these dreams was. When looking into Quantum Physic subjects which she knew nothing about, Lena was fascinated to learn about the controversial frequencies of the Universe and that some crystals here on earth vibrate at the same frequency and that there is so much we do not know when you break matter down to its smallest particles if that is even possible and the theory of relativity. It appears that we are all made up of energy.

We are all from the same energy that was present when the Universe was created. We are all connected in theory by Quantum Entanglement which is when particles link up, even if they're far apart. It gives us a deep connection in the universe and the fabric of time. Some think this connection could be part of a global consciousness field. Ancient sites like Machu Picchu might have used this for healing and spiritual goals. It is an area rich with Quartz which vibrates at its own energy frequency. So, if energy is neither created nor destroyed, where is all the energy that makes life in the Universe? Can science match the frequency of Crystals to move freely in time and space? If we could, what would happen if we changed the future or the past? Or do we need to prevent any manipulations of time.

Lena continued her schooling and graduated from high school. She went to University in California and studied and received a degree in cultural anthropology. Her passion was still her chasing her dreams. After university, she felt fortunate to have been chosen to be part of a team to travel to Peru to continue research into the Nazca Lines and high energy readings that are found in the different mountainous regions. Lena's story changes from here and she set out on a quest to search for a meaning to her dreams, meeting those who would help and those that would try to exploit her for the powers she was given in the crystal caves. She meets many good people and some who will try to exploit her discovery of what the Ancients had hidden for all these years. Lena was soon to learn that of a power she has and that she is one of the chosen ones since the time of her birth.

Contents

Chapter 1: The Dream That Stopped Time

Lena jolted upright, her breath ragged as her heart pounded against her ribcage. For a moment, the world felt hazy, her mind trapped in the space between sleep and wakefulness. She scanned her surroundings: pale blue walls, posters of constellations and distant places, and the soft glow of her bedside lamp. Slowly, reality began to reassert itself, but the dream's grip lingered—sharp and unrelenting.

It had happened again. The crystal cave. The glowing clock. The hum.

Shoving her blankets aside, Lena swung her legs over the edge of the bed, her feet meeting the cool wooden floor. A chill ran through her as vivid images of the cave filled her mind. The walls shimmered with countless crystals, each radiating a soft, otherworldly light. At the center was the clock—a magnificent, pulsating crystal suspended midair, as if held aloft by an unseen force. Unlike ordinary clocks, it didn't tick. Yet, Lena had felt it controlling time itself, stretching and twisting it around her like it was waiting for her to act.

But this dream had been different.

The hum had always been there—a deep, resonant vibration that filled the air—but now it felt alive. It wasn't just a sound anymore; it was a presence, thrumming within her chest. It wasn't external. It was part of her, a frequency she couldn't escape.

Lena rubbed her temples, trying to shake the lingering sensation. "It's just a dream," she whispered to herself, but her voice lacked conviction. For as long as she could remember, these dreams had haunted her, growing more vivid with each passing year. As a child, she thought they were fragments of an overactive imagination, fueled by bedtime stories and her love of mysteries. But now, at twelve years old, they felt like something else—like a puzzle she was destined to solve.

The shrill beep of her alarm clock shattered her thoughts, jolting her further from sleep. She slapped the off button and sighed. **6:45 a.m.** Time to face another Monday.

She shuffled to the mirror, catching her reflection. Her curly brown hair was a frizzy mess, and faint dark circles clung under her hazel eyes. She looked as tired as she felt, but after nights like that, who wouldn't be?

"Lena!" her mom called from downstairs, her voice laced with impatience. "If you don't get moving, you'll miss the bus!"

"Coming!" Lena yelled back, though her feet stayed planted for another moment. She glanced at her desk—strewn with notebooks, pencils, and an unfinished Social Studies assignment. The blank page taunted her. She hadn't even started. Every time she tried to focus, her thoughts drifted to the crystal cave, the glowing clock, and the unshakable hum.

With a resigned sigh, she grabbed her school uniform from the back of her chair and dressed quickly. Her movements were mechanical, her mind still lost in the dream. She wanted to tell someone—her mom, maybe, or her best friend Rachel—but how could she explain something so strange? It wasn't just a dream anymore. It was in her chest, buzzing and alive.

It was real.

Downstairs, the warm smell of butter and syrup filled the air as her mom flipped pancakes on the stove. Normally, Lena would have been thrilled, but today she simply poked at her food, dragging her fork through the syrup and letting the pancakes grow cold.

Her mom frowned, sitting across from her at the table. "You've been quiet lately. Is everything okay?"

"Yeah," Lena lied, forcing herself to take a bite. It tasted like cardboard. "Just tired."

Her mom didn't look convinced. "You know, you can talk to me. If something's bothering you—"

"It's nothing," Lena interrupted, her voice sharper than she intended. She softened her tone. "Really, I'm fine."

Her mom studied her for a moment longer but let it drop.

The doorbell rang, breaking the awkward silence. Her mom wiped her hands on a towel and went to answer it. Lena barely noticed, her thoughts returning to the dream. The clock. The cave. The hum.

When her mom returned, she held a thick envelope in her hands. "This came for you," she said, her tone curious.

"For me?" Lena frowned. She rarely got mail. She took the envelope, her fingers brushing against its heavy, expensive-feeling paper. Her name was written in neat, dark ink, but there was no return address.

"What is it?" her mom asked, leaning over to peer at the envelope.

"I... don't know." Lena's hands trembled slightly as she tore it open. Inside was a single sheet of crisp, ivory-colored paper. She unfolded it and read the message written in bold, elegant script:

Lena, your destiny is tied to the crystal clock. You must seek it before it is too late. Only you can control time. Your journey begins soon. Trust the signs, and trust yourself. You are chosen.

Lena's heart raced as the buzzing in her chest flared, sharp and insistent. It was as though the words had activated something deep within her. She read the message again, her hands shaking. It didn't make sense—none of it did—but it felt… true.

"Lena? What does it say?" her mom asked, her voice tinged with concern.

Lena quickly folded the paper, hiding it from view. "It's… nothing," she stammered, her voice unsteady. "Probably a mistake."

Her mom frowned. "A mistake? Lena, that doesn't—"

"I need to go," Lena blurted, standing so quickly her chair scraped against the floor. She grabbed her bag, stuffed the letter inside, and slung it over her shoulder.

"Lena—"

"I'll be fine!" she called over her shoulder, slipping out the door and leaving her mom staring after her.

Outside, the crisp autumn air stung her cheeks, but it didn't clear her head. She clutched her bag tightly, the letter's words burning in her mind.

The clock. The cave. The hum.

It wasn't just a dream. It was real.

This rewrite maintains all the key elements of the original narrative while smoothing out any awkward phrasing, improving transitions, and enhancing the story's pacing. The tone remains true to Lena's perspective, blending her sense of confusion and determination with the mounting mystery of the crystal clock.

Lena walked quickly, her thoughts racing as she headed toward the bus stop. The quiet neighborhood felt muted, the streets lined with trees shedding their autumn leaves in shades of gold and red. Normally, she would have kicked at a stray pile of leaves or stopped to admire the crisp morning, but not today. She barely noticed the crunch beneath her sneakers or the cool breeze brushing against her cheeks.

All she could think about was the letter.

Who had sent it? How did they know about her dreams? And what did they mean by **"destiny"?** The word felt heavy, almost suffocating.

The hum in her chest grew stronger with every step, as if urging her forward. But forward where? She was just a kid. She had no idea where to start or what she was supposed to do. And yet, deep down, she knew the letter wasn't random. It wasn't some cruel joke or mistake. It was meant for her.

At the bus stop, she slumped onto the bench, her bag resting on her lap. The other kids were chatting and laughing, their voices a distant hum compared to the vibration in her chest. It felt like she was in a separate world, one where time itself had slowed just for her.

Lena glanced around, half-expecting someone to appear and explain everything, but the street was empty except for the usual cars and commuters. She reached into her bag and pulled out the letter, unfolding it carefully.

"You are chosen."

The words sent a shiver down her spine. Chosen for what? She scanned the faces of the other kids waiting for the bus, wondering if they could somehow sense the weight of what she was carrying. But they were absorbed in their own lives, oblivious to her growing turmoil.

With a screech of brakes, the school bus pulled up, breaking her thoughts. Lena climbed aboard and found an empty seat near the back. She pressed her forehead to the window as the town blurred past, her mind spinning.

The clock. The cave. The hum.

They weren't just dreams anymore. They were real, and they were connected to her in ways she didn't yet understand.

By the time the bus pulled into the school parking lot, Lena had made a decision. She didn't know where this path would lead, but she couldn't ignore it. The clock was calling her.

She had to find it.

The School Day

The school day dragged on like an eternity. Lena barely paid attention in class, her thoughts far from the chalkboard and textbooks. Mrs. Thompson, her Social Studies teacher, handed out reminders about their short story assignment, but Lena's notebook remained blank.

Every time she tried to write, her mind drifted back to the message.

At lunch, her best friend Rachel plopped down beside her, her tray loaded with pizza and fries. "You look like you've seen a ghost," Rachel said, eyeing her closely. "What's up?"

"Nothing," Lena muttered automatically, but Rachel wasn't buying it.

"Come on, spill. You've been weird all day."

Lena hesitated, her fingers tightening around her juice box. Rachel was her best friend. If anyone would understand, it was her. But how could she explain something so strange?

Finally, she sighed. "I've been having these dreams," she began, keeping her voice low. "About this… clock. And today, I got this weird letter."

Rachel's eyes widened. "A letter? From who?"

"I don't know," Lena admitted. "But it said I'm supposed to find the clock. That it's my destiny or something."

Rachel blinked, and then a grin spread across her face. "Okay, that's officially the coolest thing I've ever heard."

"It's not cool," Lena said, her voice sharper than she intended. "It's… terrifying. I don't know what it means, and I don't know what to do."

Rachel's grin faded. "Do you think it's real? Like, actually real?"

Lena nodded slowly. "I think it is."

By the time Lena got home, the buzzing in her chest had settled into a persistent hum, like a quiet engine idling beneath her ribs. She let herself in, the familiar scent of her mom's cooking wafting through the air. Normally, it would have made her smile, but today, it barely registered.

She trudged upstairs, her bag feeling heavier than usual. Shutting the door behind her, she sat at her cluttered desk and pulled out the letter again.

The words stared back at her, unchanging but no less powerful:

"Your destiny is tied to the crystal clock. You must seek it before it is too late. Only you can control time. Your journey begins soon. Trust the signs, and trust yourself. You are chosen."

Lena read it over and over, hoping the repetition would unlock some hidden meaning. How had this person—whoever they were—known about her dreams? About the clock? And what did it mean to "control time"?

The questions piled up in her mind, each one more impossible than the last.

With a frustrated sigh, she reached for her dream journal, the battered notebook she kept hidden beneath her mattress. Flipping through the pages, she found her sketches of the cave: jagged crystal walls, the glowing clock at the center, and strange patterns of light that had imprinted themselves in her memory. Next to the drawings were hurried notes she had written in the middle of the night:

"The hum feels stronger."
"The light shifts when I move closer."
"Time feels slower, like it's waiting for me."

She grabbed a pen and added a new entry:

"November 25. The letter arrived today. It knows about the clock. It says I'm chosen, but I don't know why. The hum is stronger. I feel like something is going to happen, but I don't know what."

She stared at the words, then underlined them. It wasn't much, but it felt like a small step toward figuring out the truth.

That Night

When bedtime came, Lena lay in the darkness, her dream journal tucked under her pillow and the letter folded neatly beside her. Sleep didn't come easily. Her mind replayed the dream over and over: the glowing clock, the pulsing hum, the way time seemed to bend and twist around her.

When she finally drifted off, the dream came again, vivid and all-consuming.

The cave loomed before her, hidden behind a curtain of vines. Inside, the walls shimmered with light, the crystals glowing like stars in the darkness. The hum was deafening now, vibrating through her very core.

At the center of the cave stood the clock, its radiance filling the space with warmth and power.

Lena approached cautiously, her footsteps echoing on the smooth stone floor. As she moved closer, the clock seemed to respond, its light pulsing in rhythm with her heartbeat. Her fingers trembled as she reached out, stopping just short of its glowing surface.

The hum grew louder, a symphony of sound and energy, and then—

"Find me," a voice whispered, soft yet commanding. "Find me before it's too late."

The voice sent shivers down her spine, but before she could respond, the ground shifted beneath her. The clock's light dimmed, and darkness swallowed her whole.

Lena woke with a gasp, clutching her chest as her heart pounded. The hum was still there, faint but unmistakable, like a whisper in the back of her mind.

She sat up, reaching for her journal. The voice from the dream echoed in her head:

"Find me before it's too late."

She didn't know where to start or how to follow the voice's command, but one thing was clear:

The clock was real. It was waiting for her.

And somehow, she had to find it.

Chapter 2: The Incident

Lena sat stiffly at her desk, gripping the edges of her notebook as though it were the only thing keeping her tethered to the moment. The first bell of the day had rung, signaling the start of her morning lesson, but Lena's mind was light-years away, back in the dream, in the hum-filled cave where the crystal clock glowed with an impossible light.

Her notebook lay open before her, the page starkly empty save for the hastily scribbled title at the top: *The Crystal Clock*. The words seemed to mock her, a silent accusation of her inability to bring her thoughts into focus. Mrs. Thompson's assignment had been straightforward: *Write about anything,* she'd said. "Let your imagination guide you."

Anything.

And yet, Lena had stared at the blank page for hours the night before, her pen hovering uselessly above it. She had tried to write about the clock, about the cave, about the hum that seemed to pulse through her very soul. But each time she started, her thoughts became disjointed, the buzzing inside her chest growing louder and louder until it drowned out everything else.

Around her, the classroom buzzed with life: pencils scratching against paper, notebooks flipping open, the occasional ripple of laughter from her classmates. It was the sound of normalcy, of students engaged in their tasks.

Lena barely noticed.

Her heart pounded in her chest as she stared down at the page. She wanted to write. Needed to. But every time she tried, her thoughts spiraled back to the dream, to the clock's strange, otherworldly glow, and to the message she had received in her sleep: *You are chosen.*

The words reverberated in her mind, impossibly vast and incomprehensible, as elusive as the dream itself.

"Alright, class!" Mrs. Thompson's sharp voice cut through the chatter, startling Lena out of her thoughts. The teacher clapped her hands twice, the sound reverberating in the suddenly silent room. "Let's settle down and get started. I hope you all brought your short stories today. We'll be sharing them aloud."

Lena's stomach twisted into a knot. She had forgotten—no, avoided—this part of the assignment. Her classmates' gazes flicked toward her as Mrs. Thompson's words sank in.

Mrs. Thompson scanned the room, her eyes narrowing slightly. "Who would like to go first?" she asked, looking for the inevitable volunteers.

Several hands shot into the air, their owners eager to show off. Lena shrank in her seat, willing herself to disappear. Her heart thudded against her ribs, the buzzing in her chest growing sharper, more insistent.

"Let's start with Jason," Mrs. Thompson said, motioning to the boy in the second row.

Jason strode to the front of the class, his neatly typed story in hand, and began to read. It was a classic tale of knights and dragons, complete with a daring rescue of a princess. The class clapped politely when he finished, and Jason returned to his seat with a triumphant grin.

Next came Maria, who read a whimsical piece about a talking cat that could grant wishes. The class laughed in all the right places, Maria's confidence evident in every word.

Then Darren, who delivered a dark, suspenseful story about a haunted house.

One by one, Lena's classmates took their turns, each story met with polite applause. The more they shared, the heavier Lena's notebook felt, its blank pages a silent indictment of her failure.

And then Mrs. Thompson's gaze landed on her.

"Lena," the teacher said, her voice calm but expectant. "Your turn."

Lena froze.

The hum in her chest surged, roaring to life, drowning out every sound in the room. Her fingers tightened around her notebook, her breathing shallow. She couldn't do this. Her story wasn't finished—it wasn't even started. There was nothing to share.

"Lena," Mrs. Thompson said again, her tone sharpening. "Please come to the front."

Lena's legs felt like lead as she pushed herself to her feet. Clutching her notebook like a lifeline, she walked slowly to the front of the room, the weight of her classmates' stares pressing down on her with every step.

When she reached the front, she turned to face the class. Her hands trembled as she opened the notebook to the first page, the blank lines stretching endlessly before her eyes. Her vision blurred, the pressure of the moment overwhelming.

She tried to speak, her voice catching in her throat. "I... I didn't finish," she finally admitted, her words barely audible.

The classroom erupted into whispers and muffled giggles. Lena's cheeks burned as she stared at the floor, her pulse pounding in her ears.

Mrs. Thompson's expression darkened. "You didn't finish?" she repeated, her voice heavy with disapproval. "This was a simple assignment, Lena. Why didn't you complete it?"

"I…" Lena hesitated, the words refusing to come. How could she explain that the assignment had felt impossible? That every time she tried to write, her thoughts were consumed by the dream, by the clock, by the hum that seemed to vibrate through her entire being?

"I tried," she said finally, her voice trembling.

"Not hard enough," Mrs. Thompson said, crossing her arms. Her tone was cold, clipped. "You're in Grade 6 now, Lena. This kind of behavior is unacceptable. Tomorrow, I expect you to have your story completed and ready to share. Do you understand?"

"Yes, Mrs. Thompson," Lena mumbled, her head bowed in shame.

"Good. You may sit down."

Lena turned and walked back to her desk, her classmates' eyes following her every move. The whispers and stifled laughter seemed louder than ever, a wall of sound pressing against her ears. She slid into her seat, clutching her notebook tightly.

The hum in her chest throbbed, sharp and painful, as though protesting the entire ordeal.

After School

The rest of the day passed in a fog. Lena barely registered the lessons, her mind too consumed by the humiliation that clung to her like a second skin.

When the final bell rang, she bolted from the classroom, her steps quick and unsteady. Outside, the crisp autumn air hit her like a slap, but it did little to clear her head. She walked home slowly, her thoughts swirling in an endless loop.

The scene in the classroom replayed in her mind over and over again: the whispers, the laughter, Mrs. Thompson's stern voice. The weight of failure pressed heavily on her chest.

By the time she reached her house, her stomach was in knots. She hesitated at the front door, remembering Mrs. Thompson's promise to call. Her mom would know by now.

Taking a deep breath, Lena stepped inside. The house was quiet, save for the faint clatter of dishes coming from the kitchen.

"Lena?" her mom's voice called. "Can you come in here?"

Lena dropped her backpack by the stairs and trudged into the kitchen. Her mom was seated at the table, a cup of tea in her hands. She looked up as Lena entered, her expression calm but serious.

"Mrs. Thompson called," her mom said evenly. "She told me you didn't finish your assignment."

Lena nodded, her gaze fixed on the floor. "I'm sorry," she whispered. "I tried, but… I couldn't."

Her mom set down her tea and sighed. "Lena, this isn't like you. You're usually so responsible. What happened?"

Lena hesitated, the weight of the truth pressing against her. How could she explain the dreams? The hum? The clock? It all sounded so ridiculous, even to her.

"I don't know," she said finally, her voice small. "I just… I couldn't."

Her mom studied her for a long moment before nodding. "Alright," she said gently. "But you'll need to finish it tonight. I'll sit with you if you need help."

Lena nodded, her chest tight. "Okay," she said quietly.

Her mom gave her a small, encouraging smile. "You'll figure it out. I know you will."

That Night

Lena's mom eventually left her to work alone, trusting her daughter's quiet determination. The soft clink of pots and pans in the kitchen faded into the background as Lena stared at her journal. The hum inside her chest ebbed and flowed, an almost hypnotic rhythm that seemed to guide her thoughts.

With a deep breath, she picked up her pen again. This time, the act of writing felt different—less like forcing the words onto the page and more like letting them come to her.

The cave shimmered with light, each crystal reflecting an impossible array of colors. The clock stood at its center, suspended in midair as though gravity had simply given up around it. It didn't tick, didn't chime, yet it commanded time itself, its glow pulsing like a heartbeat.

The words flowed effortlessly now, as if they had been waiting for her all along. Lena paused only to glance at the clock on the wall. It was late—later than she should have been awake—but she couldn't stop. The hum had grown steadier, a soft but urgent presence that pushed her forward.

When I reached out to touch the clock, time froze. The world around me—the air, the light, the hum itself—went still. Yet I could move. I could feel the clock's energy, its power thrumming beneath my fingertips. I didn't understand it, but I knew it was calling to me. Waiting for me.

Lena set the pen down, her hands trembling. The page was full now, the story alive in a way that felt both exhilarating and terrifying. She stared at the words, her chest tight with an emotion she couldn't quite name.

The hum in her chest quieted, as though satisfied.

She closed the notebook carefully, her mind still racing. She had written something—something real, something that mattered. And tomorrow, she would share it. No matter what Mrs. Thompson or her classmates thought, she knew this story was hers.

The Dream Returns

That night, Lena lay in bed, her journal tucked safely beneath her pillow. Sleep came slowly, her thoughts too loud and restless to quiet. But eventually, exhaustion claimed her, and she drifted into the familiar embrace of the dream.

The cave stretched out before her, vast and shimmering with light. Each crystal seemed to hum with energy, their vibrations matching the steady rhythm in her chest. The clock stood at the center, its glow brighter than ever, almost blinding.

This time, Lena didn't hesitate. She stepped forward, her footsteps echoing against the smooth stone floor. The hum grew louder with each step, resonating through her body, filling her with a sense of purpose she couldn't fully explain.

When she reached the clock, its light pulsed in time with her heartbeat. She reached out, her fingers trembling, and touched its surface.

The world around her exploded into light and sound. The hum became a symphony, a chorus of energy that seemed to vibrate through every particle of her being. She saw flashes of images—people she didn't recognize, places she had never been, moments that felt both foreign and deeply familiar.

The voice returned, soft yet commanding.

"Find me. Before it's too late."

Lena tried to respond, but the words caught in her throat. The light from the clock grew brighter, enveloping her completely. She felt weightless, untethered, as though she were floating through time itself.

And then, suddenly, the ground beneath her shifted. The dream collapsed into darkness, and she was falling, tumbling into the void.

The Awakening

Lena woke with a gasp, her heart pounding. The hum in her chest was back, steady and insistent, as though the clock had left a piece of itself behind in her waking world.

She sat up, clutching the journal in her lap. Her hands were shaking, but she didn't feel afraid. The dream had been more vivid than ever, its message clearer than it had ever been.

"Find me before it's too late."

Lena didn't know where to begin or how to follow the voice's command, but she knew one thing for certain: the clock was real. It wasn't just a dream, and it wasn't just a story. It was waiting for her.

She glanced at the notebook on her desk, the pages filled with her story about the clock. Tomorrow, she would share it with her class. But tonight, she had a different mission. She flipped open her dream journal, her pen moving quickly as she recorded every detail of the dream.

The Next Day

When Lena walked into class the next morning, she felt a strange mix of nerves and determination. The memory of Mrs. Thompson's disapproval still lingered, but the hum in her chest was stronger, steadier. It gave her courage.

As the other students filed in, she kept her eyes on her notebook, reviewing her story one last time. The words felt solid, unshakable. This wasn't just an assignment—it was a part of her.

When Mrs. Thompson called her name, Lena rose from her seat and walked to the front of the room. Her classmates' eyes followed her, some curious, others dismissive. She could feel the weight of their judgment, but it didn't matter.

She opened her notebook, her hands trembling slightly, and began to read.

Her voice was quiet at first, hesitant. But as the words filled the room, she found her rhythm. She described the cave, the crystals, the hum that seemed to pulse through the air. She spoke of the clock, its impossible glow, and the way time froze when she touched it.

As Lena read, the room remained silent. The usual whispers and giggles were absent, replaced by a tense stillness. She felt a flicker of pride—until Mrs. Thompson walked toward her, her expression hard.

Halfway through Lena's story, the teacher snatched the notebook out of her hands.

"Where did you get this story?" Mrs. Thompson's voice was sharp, accusatory.

Lena blinked, stunned. "I wrote it," she said, her voice steady despite the knot in her stomach. "Last night. My mom was with me."

Mrs. Thompson's eyes narrowed, her lips thinning into a line. "Lying is unacceptable," she snapped.

Before Lena could respond, Mrs. Thompson raised her hand and slapped her across the face.

The classroom gasped. The sound of the slap echoed in the silent room, reverberating like a shockwave. Tears stung Lena's eyes, but she refused to let them fall. Her cheek burned, but the humiliation cut deeper than the physical pain.

"It's not a lie," Lena said quietly, her voice trembling with a mix of anger and defiance. "It's my story."

Mrs. Thompson didn't respond. She turned sharply and strode back to her desk, leaving Lena standing at the front of the room, her notebook clutched to her chest. The classroom was suffocatingly silent, the weight of what had just happened hanging heavy in the air.

Lena returned to her seat, her hands shaking. She felt humiliated, furious, and strangely relieved all at once. The sting on her cheek was nothing compared to the fire burning inside her.

She knew, with every fiber of her being, that she wasn't going to back down. The clock was real. The hum was real. And she was going to find it.

No matter what.

The house was eerily silent when Lena returned that afternoon, her movements mechanical as she dropped her backpack by the door and trudged upstairs. It wasn't the kind of comforting silence that usually greeted her—a quietude that gave her space to decompress from the chaos of middle school. This silence was heavy, oppressive, and seemed to grow louder with each step she took.

Her mom had peeked out from the kitchen as Lena slammed the door behind her. She had seen her daughter's hunched shoulders, her stormy face, the way her fingers clutched her notebook like it was a lifeline. There was something about Lena's body language that stopped her from asking questions. She decided not to press her, letting the quiet settle as Lena retreated to her room.

Lena barely managed a mumbled, "Hi," before closing her bedroom door and locking it.

She now sat on the edge of her bed, the same notebook in her trembling hands—the one Mrs. Thompson had snatched away in front of the entire class. Its pages felt heavier than ever, as if they carried the weight of her humiliation and the disbelief of everyone who had heard her story.

The sting of Mrs. Thompson's slap had faded from her cheek, but the words that had followed it were fresh and sharp, repeating themselves over and over in her mind like a cruel refrain.

"You didn't write this. You're lying."

Lena's fingers tightened around the notebook, her knuckles whitening under the strain. She wasn't lying. She *knew* that with every fiber of her being. Yet, Mrs. Thompson's disbelief had done more than embarrass her; it had planted a tiny, insidious seed of doubt in her mind.

What if Mrs. Thompson was right?

She shook her head violently, rejecting the thought. No, she wasn't lying. The story was hers. The clock, the cave, the hum—they were as much a part of her as her own heartbeat.

Opening the notebook to the page she had written the night before, Lena stared down at the words. They stared back at her, vivid and alive, like fragments of the dream that had haunted her for so many nights.

The clock. The cave. The hum.

Tears pricked the corners of her eyes and spilled over before she could stop them. She hunched over the notebook, her shoulders trembling as silent sobs wracked her small frame.

She had tried. She had poured herself into the story, hoping—*praying*—that it would help her make sense of everything. She had thought that maybe, just maybe, sharing it with someone else would make the weight of it all a little easier to bear.

Instead, she had been met with disbelief and ridicule.

Her classmates had smirked and whispered. Mrs. Thompson had called her a liar.

And the slap—humiliating, degrading—had felt like a cruel punctuation mark to the worst day of her life.

Lena felt so small, so utterly alone.

But even in the midst of her tears, she felt it. The hum. Soft at first, almost imperceptible, but growing stronger with every shaky breath she took.

The hum wasn't just a feeling. It was alive. It was real. And it was waiting for her.

She wiped her face with the sleeve of her sweater, taking a deep, shuddering breath. She didn't know why this was happening to her or what the clock wanted, but she *knew* one thing for certain: it wasn't just a story.

It was real.

And one day, the world would believe her.

A Soft Knock

The knock on her door was quiet, hesitant.

"Lena?" her mom's voice filtered through the wood, gentle and concerned. "Can I come in?"

Lena didn't answer. She didn't trust herself to speak without breaking into sobs again. After a moment of silence, the door creaked open. Her mom stepped inside, her gaze softening the instant she saw Lena curled up on the bed, the notebook clutched to her chest like a shield.

Her mom crossed the room and sat down beside her. She didn't speak right away, just placed a comforting hand on Lena's shoulder.

"I got a call from Mrs. Thompson," she said quietly. "She told me what happened."

Lena stiffened, bracing herself for the lecture that was surely coming. But her mom didn't sound angry.

"She said you didn't finish your story," her mom continued, her voice calm. "That you made up some elaborate excuse. But I know you, Lena. I know you wouldn't just make something up. I saw your story. It was finished for your presentation. Do you want to tell me what's going on?"

For a long moment, Lena didn't say anything. She stared down at the notebook in her hands, tracing the edges of the page with her fingers. Finally, she whispered, "She doesn't believe me."

Her mom tilted her head. "Believe you about what?"

"About the clock," Lena said, her voice trembling. "About the dreams. About… everything."

Her mom frowned, her concern deepening. "What clock?"

Lena hesitated, then opened the notebook to the first page. The crystal clock stared back at them, its intricate details rendered in careful strokes of pencil.

"This," Lena said, her voice barely audible. "It's in my dreams. Every night. It's… it's calling me."

Her mom studied the drawing, her brow furrowing. "It's beautiful," she said slowly. "And you dream about this often?"

"Every night," Lena said. "But it's not just a dream, Mom. I can feel it. Here." She pressed a hand to her chest, where the hum vibrated steadily. "It's real. I know it sounds crazy, but it's real."

Her mom didn't respond right away. She looked at Lena, her expression thoughtful, searching. Finally, she said, "Lena, sometimes our dreams are trying to tell us something. Maybe this clock—this cave—it's a symbol for something you're going through. Something you're trying to figure out."

Lena shook her head, frustration bubbling up inside her. "It's not just a symbol," she said. "It's real. I can feel it."

Her mom hesitated, then nodded. "Alright," she said gently. "If you believe it's real, then we'll figure it out together. But for now, why don't you focus on writing it down? You've already started. Maybe putting more of it into words will help you understand it better."

Lena wasn't sure it would help, but she nodded anyway. Her mom gave her a small, encouraging smile before standing up and leaving the room.

Writing the Truth

The notebook sat open in her lap, its blank pages staring back at her. Lena took a deep breath, her pen poised above the paper.

She wrote the title at the top of the page in shaky, determined handwriting:

The Crystal Clock.

As soon as the words were on the page, the hum in her chest grew warmer, steadier, as if it were responding to her actions. Slowly, carefully, Lena began to put the dream into words.

The cave is vast, shimmering with light that seems to come from everywhere and nowhere. The air hums with energy, vibrating like a heartbeat. At the center of the cave stands the clock. It's not like any clock I've ever seen. It's made of crystal, glowing faintly, its surface smooth and cold. When I touch it, everything stops. Time freezes. I can move while the rest of the world stands still.

She paused, her pen hovering over the page. The hum in her chest was growing stronger now, insistent but not overwhelming. She closed her eyes, letting the memory of the dream flood her mind.

I don't know why I'm the only one who can move. I don't know why the clock is calling me. But I can feel it. It's real. It's waiting for me.

When Lena looked at what she had written, the page was full. She was realizing how much this was becoming part of her. She had never written so much so quickly. It was as if the words had been waiting for her all along, waiting for her to let them out.

The hum in her chest quieted, as though satisfied.

She closed the notebook carefully, her heart pounding. She had written something—something real, something that mattered.

No matter what Mrs. Thompson or her classmates thought, Lena knew this story was hers.

Resolve

That night, Lena tucked the notebook under her pillow and lay awake, staring at the ceiling. The hum was still there, a quiet but steady presence in her chest. It didn't feel overwhelming anymore. It felt like a guide, pushing her forward.

She didn't know what the clock wanted or why it had chosen her, but she knew she had to find out.

As she drifted off to sleep, the dream came again, clearer and more vivid than her previous dreams.

The cave stretched out before her, vast and shimmering with light. The crystals hummed softly, their vibrations resonating with the rhythm in her chest. The clock stood at the center, its glow brighter than ever, almost blinding.

This time, Lena didn't hesitate.

She stepped forward, her footsteps echoing against the smooth stone floor. The hum grew louder with each step, filling her with a sense of purpose she couldn't explain.

When she reached the clock, its light pulsed in time with her heartbeat. She reached out, her fingers trembling, and touched its surface.

The world around her exploded into light and sound. The hum became a symphony, a chorus of energy that seemed to vibrate through every particle of her being.

And then the voice came, soft yet commanding.

"Find me. Before it's too late."

The light grew brighter, enveloping her completely. She felt weightless, untethered, as though she were floating through time itself.

And then she woke up.

The hum in her chest was stronger than ever.

The clock wasn't just a story.

It was waiting for her.

And Lena was ready to find it.

Chapter 4: The Path of Discovery

The years had passed swiftly, and now Lena stood on the threshold of adulthood. Senior year in high school should have felt monumental, the culmination of years of growth, friendships, and accomplishments. But for Lena, it was merely a backdrop—a chapter that she was ready to close so she could move forward to what truly mattered.

The crystal clock still visited her dreams, though less frequently than it had when she was younger. When it did appear, it was more vivid than ever, each detail of the shimmering cave and the humming energy etched into her mind with startling clarity. The hum, however, never left her waking life. It remained a steady undercurrent in her chest, resonating with a quiet intensity that was impossible to ignore.

Lena's curiosity about the clock had grown alongside her, becoming more urgent as the years passed. What had once been a childhood mystery had transformed into a burning desire for answers. Why did the clock choose her? Why did it feel so real, so connected to her very being? And what was it trying to tell her?

The Weight of Questions

The final bell of the day echoed through the school hallways, a sound that usually signified freedom. For Lena, it was little more than background noise. She slid her books into her worn canvas bag and slipped past her classmates, who were already making plans for the weekend. Their chatter and laughter washed over her like waves, but she barely noticed.

High school had once felt like a labyrinth of whispers and stares, a place where her "strange" interests had made her a target of ridicule. But by Grade 12, Lena had learned to carry herself with quiet confidence. The whispers had faded as her peers grew more preoccupied with their own lives, and she had found solace in her independence.

Still, her world felt small compared to the questions that consumed her thoughts. Graduation was just months away, but Lena wasn't thinking about prom or college applications. Her focus was elsewhere, on the mysteries that had defined her life for as long as she could remember.

She shouldered her bag and headed toward the library, her sanctuary. It had become her safe haven over the years, a quiet place where she could lose herself in books and theories that spoke to the questions no one else seemed to understand.

A Place of Solace

The library was nearly empty when Lena arrived, the soft hum of the fluorescent lights and the faint rustle of pages creating a soothing ambiance. She made her way to her usual corner table, tucked away near the back shelves where few students ventured.

Lena's notebook was already thick with sketches and notes about the crystal clock. Over the years, she had filled its pages with meticulous drawings of the cave, detailed diagrams of the clock's structure, and countless questions scrawled in the margins.

Today, she opened a new book—an advanced text on quantum mechanics that she had borrowed earlier that week. The equations and theories were dense, far beyond what most high school seniors would attempt to tackle, but Lena had grown used to navigating complex material.

As she skimmed the pages, her mind wandered back to the clock. She could almost feel its glow, the way its energy seemed to pulse in rhythm with her heartbeat. No matter how much she read or how many theories she explored, the answers always seemed just out of reach, like a word on the tip of her tongue.

Lena sighed, tapping her pen against the notebook. "Why me?" she muttered under her breath. "Why do I feel this way?"

The hum in her chest vibrated gently, as if responding to her unspoken questions.

An Unexpected Guide

"Late again, I see," a familiar voice said, pulling Lena from her thoughts.

She looked up to see Mrs. Harrison, the school librarian, standing at the edge of her table. With her sharp eyes and soft demeanor, Mrs. Harrison had become something of an enigma to Lena. She was always there, quietly observing, her presence comforting yet mysterious.

Lena offered a faint smile. "I guess I've been spending a lot of time here."

Mrs. Harrison tilted her head, her gaze drifting to the open book in front of Lena. It was filled with diagrams of quantum particles and dense equations.

"Quantum mechanics?" Mrs. Harrison asked, raising an eyebrow. "That's ambitious for a senior."

Lena hesitated, unsure how much she should share. But something about Mrs. Harrison's steady, understanding gaze made her feel safe.

"It's not just for school," Lena admitted after a pause. "I'm trying to figure something out. Something that doesn't make sense."

Mrs. Harrison pulled out the chair across from Lena and sat down, folding her hands neatly on the table. "Why don't you tell me about it?"

Lena glanced around the library, ensuring no one else was within earshot. Then, taking a deep breath, she began.

"For years, I've been having these dreams. About a cave filled with crystals and a clock at its center. It's not like any clock I've ever seen. When I touch it, time stops. Everything freezes, but I can still move. It feels… real. Like it's trying to tell me something."

Mrs. Harrison didn't laugh or dismiss her words. Instead, she leaned forward, her expression thoughtful. "And you think this clock is connected to quantum physics?"

Lena nodded, her voice quickening with urgency. "I don't know for sure, but I've been reading about time, energy, relativity. There's this hum I feel in my chest, like it's vibrating with… something. It's not just a dream. I know it's not."

For a long moment, Mrs. Harrison was silent, her gaze searching Lena's face. Then she smiled. "It sounds like you're asking some very important questions. And I think you're right—there's more to time and energy than most people realize. Would you like some help sorting through all this?"

Lena blinked, stunned. "You mean it?"

Mrs. Harrison nodded. "Before I became a librarian, I was a physicist. I spent years studying the principles of quantum mechanics and energy fields. If you're serious about this—and I believe you are—I'd be happy to guide you."

Relief washed over Lena, followed by a spark of excitement. For the first time, she felt like she wasn't alone in her search for answers.

"Thank you," she said, her voice earnest. "I don't even know where to start."

"Then let's start with the basics," Mrs. Harrison said. "Have you heard of quantum entanglement?"

Diving into the Unknown

Over the next several weeks, Lena's afternoons transformed into a whirlwind of diagrams, theories, and animated discussions with Mrs. Harrison. The librarian guided her through the tangled world of quantum mechanics, explaining concepts like particle duality, energy fields, and the elusive nature of time itself.

"Quantum entanglement," Mrs. Harrison explained one evening, "is the idea that particles can become linked in such a way that, no matter how far apart they are, their states remain connected. It's as though they share an invisible bond, one that transcends space and time."

Lena leaned forward, her mind racing. "So, if everything is connected, could time be connected too? Could it be… manipulated?"

Mrs. Harrison smiled. "That's one interpretation. Time isn't as rigid as we once thought. According to Einstein's theory of relativity, time is fluid—affected by speed, gravity, and perspective. If the clock in your dream is tied to time itself, it could be tapping into these principles."

Lena scribbled furiously in her notebook, her thoughts tumbling over one another. "And the hum I feel—it's like energy. Could it be connected to the clock? To time?"

"It could," Mrs. Harrison said. "Energy fields permeate the universe, and some believe they're tied to the fabric of reality itself. Perhaps this hum you feel is part of a larger force, one that connects you to the clock."

The hum in Lena's chest swelled, as if affirming Mrs. Harrison's words. For the first time, she felt like she was beginning to understand. The clock wasn't just a dream. It was part of something far bigger—a web of energy and time that she was somehow connected to.

Finding Purpose

As the weeks passed, Lena's confidence grew. Her understanding of quantum physics deepened, and with it came a sense of purpose. She no longer felt lost or overwhelmed. The pieces of the puzzle were starting to fit together, and the crystal clock was at the center of it all.

One evening, as Lena packed up her books, Mrs. Harrison stopped her at the library door.

"Lena," she said, her voice soft but firm, "I want you to remember something. The universe is full of mysteries—things we can't always explain. But the answers are out there, waiting for those who are brave enough to seek them. Trust your instincts. They'll guide you where you need to go."

Lena nodded, her heart swelling with gratitude. "Thank you," she said. "For everything."

Mrs. Harrison smiled. "You're welcome. But remember, this journey is yours. I can only point you in the right direction. The rest is up to you."

A New Beginning

The cool evening air wrapped around Lena like a calming balm, soothing the tension that had built up during her hours in the library. The fading sunlight painted the horizon in streaks of amber and violet, a serene contrast to the whirlwind of thoughts in her mind. For once, the hum in her chest didn't feel like a burden; it felt purposeful, steady, and reassuring.

As she walked home, her bag weighed down with notebooks and textbooks, Lena replayed the conversations she'd had with Mrs. Harrison over the past few weeks. The librarian's guidance had opened new doors in Lena's understanding of quantum mechanics and energy. Concepts like quantum entanglement, time dilation, and the fluidity of time no longer felt abstract—they felt like pieces of a puzzle she was destined to solve.

But one question loomed above all others: **Why her?**

The hum wasn't random. The dreams weren't ordinary. Lena was certain now that the crystal clock wasn't just a figment of her imagination. It was real, and somehow, it was connected to her. But what did it want? And why had it chosen her?

Home and Reflection

When Lena arrived home, her mom was in the kitchen, the aroma of freshly baked bread wafting through the air. It was a comforting, familiar scene, but tonight it felt almost surreal. Lena's mind was miles away, tangled in thoughts of the cave, the clock, and the inexplicable pull she felt toward them.

"Hey, sweetheart," her mom said, glancing up from the stove. "You're home late again. Still working on that project?"

Lena hesitated. Her mom had always been supportive, but she wasn't sure how much to share. Would she understand? Or would she brush it off as a teenager's overactive imagination?

"Yeah," Lena said finally, setting her bag down by the door. "It's... complicated."

Her mom gave her a knowing smile. "Well, dinner will be ready soon. Why don't you wash up and take a break? You've been working so hard lately."

"Thanks, Mom," Lena said, forcing a smile. She headed upstairs, her heart heavy with the weight of her secrets.

In her room, Lena unpacked her bag and spread her notebooks across the bed. Pages filled with sketches, equations, and theories stared back at her, a testament to weeks of relentless effort. But no matter how much she studied, she couldn't shake the feeling that she was missing something—something crucial.

She opened her dream journal, flipping to the latest entry. The drawing of the crystal clock was more detailed than ever, every facet of its glowing surface etched with precision. Beneath the drawing, she had scrawled a single line:

"The answers are in the hum."

Lena placed a hand over her chest, feeling the steady vibration that had been her constant companion for as long as she could remember. The hum was more than a sensation—it was a signal, a guide. She closed her eyes, focusing on its rhythm, letting it fill her mind.

Images began to form behind her closed eyelids: the shimmering walls of the cave, the glowing crystals, the clock pulsing with energy. But this time, there was something new—a path leading deeper into the cave, its end obscured by shadow.

Lena's eyes snapped open, her heart racing. The vision had felt so real, so vivid, that for a moment she wondered if it had been more than just her imagination. Was the hum trying to show her something? Was it leading her toward the truth?

Reaching Out

The next day, Lena couldn't concentrate in class. Her teachers' voices faded into the background as her mind wandered back to the vision. She needed answers, and there was only one person she trusted to help her: Mrs. Harrison.

As soon as the final bell rang, Lena headed straight for the library. Mrs. Harrison was at her usual spot behind the desk, sorting through a stack of books. She looked up and smiled when she saw Lena.

"Back so soon?" Mrs. Harrison asked, her tone light but curious.

"I need your help," Lena said, her voice urgent. "I think… I think I'm onto something."

Mrs. Harrison set the books aside and gestured for Lena to follow her to the study area. Once they were seated, Lena pulled out her dream journal and opened it to the page with the drawing of the clock.

"This is what I see in my dreams," Lena began, her words tumbling out in a rush. "But last night, I saw something new—a path leading deeper into the cave. It felt so real, like the hum was trying to show me where to go."

Mrs. Harrison studied the drawing, her expression thoughtful. "You believe the hum is guiding you?"

Lena nodded. "It's not just a feeling. It's like… it's like a map, or a signal. And I think it's connected to this clock. But I don't know how to follow it."

Mrs. Harrison leaned back in her chair, her gaze distant. "If the hum is a signal, it might be tied to a specific frequency—something that resonates with you on a physical and emotional level. Have you ever tried to track it?"

"Track it?" Lena repeated, confused.

Mrs. Harrison nodded. "Using sound, or vibrations. There are tools that can measure frequencies. If we can identify the hum's frequency, it might give us a clue about its source."

Lena's mind raced. The idea was both thrilling and daunting. Could it really be that simple? Could a tool help her unravel the mystery that had haunted her for years?

Experimenting with Frequencies

That evening, Mrs. Harrison loaned Lena a small tuning fork and a portable frequency analyzer—a device she had used during her years as a physicist. "Start with one tuning fork," Mrs. Harrison had advised. "Strike it, and see if its vibration aligns with the hum in your chest. Continue until one does. If it does, use the analyzer to record the frequency."

At home, Lena sat at her desk, the tuning fork in one hand and the analyzer in the other. One after another she repeated the process. She took a deep breath, feeling the hum in her chest, and struck the fork against the edge of the desk. The fork vibrated, emitting a soft, steady tone.

For a moment, nothing happened. But then, to Lena's astonishment, the hum in her chest seemed to respond, its rhythm aligning with the vibration of the tuning fork. The sensation was almost electric, a jolt of energy that made her heart race.

She quickly held the analyzer up to the fork, watching as the device recorded the frequency. The number that appeared on the screen was unfamiliar, but it felt significant—like a key to a lock she had been trying to open for years.

The Connection

The next day, Lena showed the recorded frequency to Mrs. Harrison, who studied it with a mixture of curiosity and excitement. "This is remarkable," she said. "This frequency is unusually high—far beyond the range of typical human perception. Whatever this hum is, it's not random."

"What does it mean?" Lena asked, her voice barely above a whisper.

Mrs. Harrison hesitated. "I don't know for certain. But if the hum is tied to the clock in your dreams, it might be a form of communication—something or someone trying to reach you. Hypothetically speaking that is"

The thought sent a shiver down Lena's spine. Communication. The idea was both thrilling and terrifying. If the hum was a message, what was it trying to say? And who—or what—was sending it?

A New Resolve

As Lena walked home that evening, the weight of the mystery felt heavier than ever. But for the first time, she felt like she was making progress. The hum, the clock, the cave—it was all connected, and she was closer than ever to understanding how.

The hum in her chest was steady now, its rhythm like a heartbeat. It wasn't just a sound; it was a promise. A promise that the answers were out there, waiting for her to find them.

Lena clenched her fists, her resolve hardening. She didn't know where this path would lead, but she was ready to follow it—no matter where it took her.

Chapter 5: The Dream Deepens

The dreams had changed.

What once felt like fleeting glimpses—ephemeral and fragmented—had transformed into vivid, immersive experiences that consumed Lena's nights. They weren't mere dreams anymore. Every time she closed her eyes, she wasn't simply watching; she was there, fully present in the shimmering cave, standing before the crystal clock.

The cave radiated an otherworldly light, refracted through countless crystalline formations jutting out like jagged, luminescent teeth. Each crystal seemed alive, humming faintly in harmony with the vibrations that resonated within her chest. The air carried an electric charge, so tangible Lena sometimes thought she could reach out and grasp it.

At the center of it all stood the clock.

Towering and majestic, it pulsed with an ethereal blue-white glow, its surface smooth and gleaming yet layered with intricacies that defied logic. There were no hands, no ticking, no visible gears—only a radiant, swirling energy that gave it life. It exuded a gravity that pulled Lena toward it, as if it held the essence of time itself.

Her dreams always brought her to the same moment: standing before the clock, her hand outstretched and trembling. The hum in her chest would intensify, almost unbearably so, as her fingers hovered over the clock's surface. The moment her fingertips made contact, the world around her froze.

The dripping sound of water striking crystal would stop mid-drip. The faint breeze brushing her face would halt in midair. Even the persistent hum that resonated through her waking life would become eerily still. The world was hers alone—a breathtaking yet unnerving stillness that both terrified and enthralled her.

Navigating the Stillness

At first, the sensation of frozen time overwhelmed Lena. She had stumbled through the motionless cave, her breath shallow and her movements hesitant. The unnatural stillness felt wrong, as though she had stepped outside the boundaries of existence. But over time, she began to acclimate.

There was a peculiar beauty to the stillness. The cave seemed to expand in this frozen state, revealing hidden details she hadn't noticed before: the intricate patterns in the crystals, the faint glow of symbols etched into the walls, the way the clock's energy rippled outward like invisible waves.

The more dreams she had, the more familiar she became with the cave's layout. It wasn't static—it evolved with each visit, revealing new paths and mysteries. The walls would shift, revealing hidden alcoves adorned with glowing symbols. Lena tried to memorize them, sketching them frantically in her notebook the moment she awoke.

The symbols were unlike anything she had ever seen, yet they felt ancient and significant. Some resembled Egyptian hieroglyphs, others mirrored Incan patterns, and others seemed to map the alignment of stars. They weren't just decorative; they felt like clues, pieces of a puzzle she was meant to solve.

The Voice

One night, as Lena stood before the clock, the symbols on the walls began to shimmer, their light pulsing in time with the hum in her chest. Then, she heard it: a voice.

"You are the chosen one. Protect the clock. Protect time. The balance must remain undisturbed."

The voice was distant yet powerful, resonating through the cave like a deep, reverberating echo. It jolted Lena awake, her heart pounding in her chest. She sat up in bed, the words replaying in her mind:

Protect the clock. Protect time.

She whispered the phrases to herself, committing them to memory. Who had spoken to her? Was it the clock itself? Or something else—something greater?

The words added a new weight to her dreams. If she was the "chosen one," what did that mean? What balance was she supposed to protect? And what would happen if she failed?

Searching for Answers

The morning after the dream, Lena sat at her desk, staring at her cluttered notebook. Pages filled with chaotic sketches of the cave, diagrams of the clock, and hastily scrawled notes stared back at her. The once-organized notebook had become a labyrinth of thoughts and theories.

At the top of one page, she had written: "Time, energy, and space are connected. The clock is the key to this connection. But why me?"

It was the question that haunted her the most. Why had she been chosen? What made her different from anyone else?

Her eyes lingered on a sketch of the clock, its radiant glow captured in careful pencil strokes. Below it, she had scribbled another line: "The hum is the key."

The hum had always been with her, a constant companion in her chest. It wasn't just a feeling—it was a guide, a signal. But guiding her where?

Conversations with Mrs. Harrison

Lena's search for answers often led her to Mrs. Harrison, the librarian who had become her confidant and mentor. Their discussions about quantum mechanics had reshaped Lena's understanding of the universe.

"Quantum entanglement," Mrs. Harrison had explained during one of their talks, "is the phenomenon where two particles become intrinsically linked, so much so that their states are connected, no matter how far apart they are. It's as if they're communicating instantaneously, faster than the speed of light."

Lena had leaned forward, her mind racing. "Could time work like that? Could moments in time be linked, no matter the distance?"

Mrs. Harrison had smiled knowingly. "Time, energy, particles—they're all interconnected. The challenge is understanding how that interconnectedness works."

Lena was certain the crystal clock was a manifestation of that interconnectedness. It wasn't just a symbol in her dreams; it was a bridge between the physical and the metaphysical, a gateway to understanding the fabric of the universe.

Theories and Discoveries

Back in her room, Lena opened a fresh page in her notebook and began writing her latest theory:

Time isn't linear. It's a fabric, woven from countless threads of energy. The clock doesn't just stop time—it bends it, shapes it. It exists outside the flow of normal time, anchoring it in place.

The hum in her chest seemed to respond, growing warmer and more insistent. She paused, staring at her words. If the clock truly allowed her to manipulate time, what could she do with it? Could she change the past? Glimpse the future? Rewrite reality itself?

The possibilities were endless—and terrifying. With great power came great responsibility. The voice's warning echoed in her mind: "The balance must remain undisturbed."

She shivered, closing her notebook. The weight of the clock's power was almost too much to bear. If she was meant to wield it, how could she ensure she didn't destroy the balance she was supposed to protect?

The New Dream

That night, the dream returned, sharper and more vivid than ever. The cave seemed brighter, the hum louder, the symbols on the walls glowing with an intensity that filled Lena with both awe and unease.

As she approached the clock, the symbols shifted, rearranging themselves into patterns she couldn't decipher. She reached out, her hand trembling as it hovered above the clock's surface. But before she could touch it, the voice returned.

"You must find me," it whispered, soft yet commanding. "The path begins where the sun meets the stone. Trust the hum. Trust yourself."

The voice faded, leaving Lena standing in the cave, her heart racing. When she woke, the words burned in her mind: "The sun meets the stone."

The Riddle

Lena sat at her desk, her notebook open to a fresh page. She wrote the phrase down, her thoughts racing. **The sun meets the stone.** It sounded like a riddle, something ancient and symbolic.

Could it be a real place? A specific location she was meant to find? Or was it metaphorical, a clue she needed to interpret?

Lena thought back to her studies. She had read about ancient monuments, caves, and structures built to align with celestial events—the sun illuminating specific stones during solstices, marking sacred times. Could the voice be pointing her to something like that?

She grabbed her laptop and began researching. Her search led her to articles about ancient sites: Stonehenge, Machu Picchu, the pyramids of Egypt and more. Each one held deep connections to the sun, stones, and some eluded to time itself.

But none of them felt right.

A New Path

As the night wore on, Lena's frustration grew. She leaned back in her chair, her gaze drifting to the window. The moon hung low in the sky, casting a pale glow over the rooftops. The hum in her chest pulsed steadily, as if urging her not to give up.

She closed her eyes, focusing on the rhythm of the hum. Images began to form in her mind: the shimmering cave, the glowing clock, and a beam of sunlight piercing through a crack in the cave wall, illuminating a single stone.

Lena's eyes snapped open. Her breath caught in her throat. The vision felt so real, so specific. **The sun meeting the stone wasn't just a metaphor—it was a moment.**

The cave wasn't just a dream. It was a real place.

The Decision

Lena's heart raced as the realization took hold. The cave was out there, waiting for her to find it. And she knew, deep down, that the clock was waiting too.

The path to its secrets was beginning to reveal itself.

For the first time, Lena felt ready to take the next step.

That morning, the realization still sat heavy in Lena's chest. The cave wasn't just a dream—it was real. And it was waiting for her to find it. But how? She had no map, no coordinates, and no one she could ask for help without sounding like she'd lost her mind.

Still, the voice's words echoed in her mind: **The path begins where the sun meets the stone. Trust the hum. Trust yourself.**

Sitting at her desk, Lena flipped through her notebook, the pages alive with frantic sketches and fragmented notes. One page caught her attention—her most detailed drawing of the crystal clock, surrounded by the symbols she had tried to copy from the cave walls. She stared at the shapes, willing them to reveal their secrets. The hum in her chest swelled faintly, as though urging her onward.

She leaned back in her chair, chewing on the end of her pen. "Where the sun meets the stone," she murmured to herself. Was it a place on Earth? Or something she had yet to discover in the dreams?

Her thoughts were interrupted by a knock at her bedroom door.

"Lena?" Her mother's voice was cautious, as if testing her mood. "Can I come in?"

"Yeah, sure," Lena called, quickly flipping her notebook closed.

Her mom stepped inside, holding two steaming mugs of tea. She set one on Lena's desk and perched on the edge of the bed. "You've been quiet lately," she said, her eyes soft with concern. "Is everything okay?"

Lena hesitated. She wanted to spill everything—to tell her mom about the dreams, the clock, the hum that felt like a living thing inside her. But how could she explain something she didn't fully understand herself?

"I'm fine," she said instead, forcing a smile. "Just… a lot on my mind. You know, school, graduation stuff."

Her mom didn't look convinced, but she nodded. "If you ever want to talk about it, I'm here."

"Thanks," Lena said quietly, her gaze dropping to the untouched tea on her desk.

Her mom stood, lingering for a moment as if she wanted to say more. Finally, she gave a small smile and left, closing the door softly behind her. Lena let out a breath she hadn't realized she was holding.

The hum pulsed faintly in her chest, almost like a whisper of reassurance. **You're not alone,** it seemed to say.

Seeking Clues

That afternoon, Lena decided to take a walk. The air was crisp and cool, the sun casting long shadows across the streets. She wandered aimlessly at first, her mind racing with fragments of theories and possibilities. The phrase "where the sun meets the stone" circled endlessly in her thoughts.

She found herself drawn to the park on the edge of town, a place she hadn't visited in years. It was quiet, the kind of place where time seemed to slow down. She followed the winding paths, her feet crunching on fallen leaves, until she reached a small clearing. At its center stood a weathered stone sundial, its surface worn smooth by years of exposure.

Lena stopped, her breath catching in her throat. The sun was low in the sky, its rays casting long, angled shadows across the sundial's face. **The sun meets the stone.**

She stepped closer, her heart pounding. The sundial was old, its markings faded and almost indecipherable. But something about it felt significant. She knelt down, tracing her fingers over the surface. A faint vibration hummed beneath her fingertips—not quite the same as the hum in her chest, but familiar.

The hairs on the back of her neck stood on end. This wasn't the cave. It wasn't the clock. But it was connected, somehow. She was sure of it. It was starting to feel like everything was connected in some way.

The Encounter

As she rose to her feet, a voice behind her startled her. "It's beautiful, isn't it?"

Lena spun around, her heart leaping into her throat. An elderly man stood a few feet away, his hands clasped behind his back. He wore a weathered coat and a wool cap, his eyes sharp and curious.

"I—I guess," Lena stammered, glancing back at the sundial.

The man stepped closer, his gaze thoughtful. "Not many people stop to look at it anymore. It's easy to forget the old things, isn't it? But sometimes, the old things have more to say than we realize."

Lena frowned, unsure how to respond. There was something unsettlingly perceptive about the way he spoke, as if he knew more than he was letting on.

"Do you come here often?" she asked, her voice cautious.

The man chuckled. "I've been coming here for years. This sundial… it's special, you know. Built to align perfectly with the solstice sun. When the light hits it just right, it marks a moment of perfect balance."

The word "balance" sent a chill down Lena's spine. She thought of the voice in her dream: **Protect the clock. Protect time. The balance must remain undisturbed.**

"Do you know who built it?" she asked, her curiosity piqued.

The man shook his head. "No one really knows. It's been here longer than anyone can remember. Some say it was placed here for a reason—an anchor, of sorts."

"An anchor?" Lena repeated, her pulse quickening.

He nodded, his gaze steady. "To hold things in place. To remind us of what's important."

Before Lena could ask what he meant, he tipped his hat and began to walk away, his steps slow and deliberate. "Take care, young lady," he called over his shoulder. "Sometimes, the answers we seek are closer than we think."

Lena watched him go, her mind racing. Who was he? And how did he seem to know exactly what she was searching for? Was this another message or was she trying to hard to make sense of something so obscure and distant.

The last bell of the school year rang, its chime reverberating down the crowded hallways of Roosevelt High. Lena stood at the entrance to the gymnasium, her blue cap balanced precariously on her head, her golden tassel swaying gently with each breath. The buzz of excitement was everywhere—laughter, shouts, the hum of conversations layered over the distant strains of the marching band warming up outside.

All around her were the faces of classmates she'd known for years. Some she had shared laughter with, others were distant memories of passing interactions. The energy in the room was palpable, but Lena felt a strange disconnection. Where others were carried away by the moment, caught up in the excitement of graduation, Lena stood still, her thoughts swirling far from the gymnasium.

Graduation.

The word lingered in her mind like a mantra, a marker of the end of one chapter and the uncertain beginning of another. The thought should have been exhilarating, but for Lena, it carried a strange weight. High school was over. The years of whispered judgments, of feeling out of place, were behind her. But the dreams—the pull of the crystal clock—had only grown stronger. It was as if the closer she got to stepping into adulthood, the louder the hum in her chest became.

She adjusted the cap on her head and walked toward her assigned seat among the rows of folding chairs set up for the ceremony. The air buzzed with the sound of gowns swishing and excited murmurs. The class valedictorian stood on stage, adjusting the microphone, preparing for their speech. Lena barely noticed. Her mind was elsewhere.

The ceremony itself was a blur. Speeches about perseverance, about friendship, about embracing the future came and went, their words bouncing off her without much impact. She clapped politely when prompted, stood for the national anthem, and dutifully walked across the stage when her name was called. The principal handed her the diploma, and the crowd erupted in cheers.

She forced a smile as she shook his hand, her movements automatic, her mind already racing ahead. *Berkeley.* That was her next step. The University of California, Berkeley, where she would study cultural anthropology on a scholarship she had worked tirelessly to earn.

Her choice had been deliberate, almost inevitable. Lena had always been fascinated by the stories of ancient civilizations— their myths, their rituals, their understanding of the cosmos. In them, she found echoes of her dreams, glimpses of answers to the questions that haunted her. The crystal clock was more than a dream, she was certain of it. But even if it was real, she didn't know where to look for it. It was a thread connecting her to something ancient, something powerful, and perhaps Berkeley would help her unravel that mystery.

After the ceremony, the crowd spilled out of the gymnasium and onto the school grounds. Parents hugged their children, friends posed for pictures in their caps and gowns, and laughter filled the air. Lena lingered near the back of the crowd, her smile tight as she endured a few obligatory congratulations from classmates she barely knew.

Her mother found her quickly, pulling her into a tight embrace. "I'm so proud of you, Lena," she said, her voice thick with emotion. "You've worked so hard for this. You deserve every bit of it."

"Thanks, Mom," Lena murmured, her arms tightening around her mother. The familiar warmth of her mom's presence grounded her, even if her thoughts still swirled elsewhere.

"I can't believe you're heading to California in just a couple of months," her mother continued, stepping back to look at her daughter. "Berkeley is such a big step. But I know you're going to do amazing things there."

Lena nodded, her heart swelling with a mix of pride and uncertainty. She wanted to believe her mother's words, to feel the excitement that everyone else seemed to feel, but there was a restlessness inside her, a voice that whispered, *this is just the beginning.*

As the celebrations continued around her, Lena slipped away from the crowd and made her way to the library. The quiet sanctuary had always been her refuge, a place where she could escape the noise of the world and dive into her research. She found Mrs. Harrison at her usual spot near the back shelves, organizing a stack of returned books.

"Well, if it isn't our newest graduate," Mrs. Harrison said warmly as Lena approached. "You look all grown up in that cap and gown."

Lena chuckled softly, tugging at the edges of her gown. "It feels a little surreal."

"Big moments often do," Mrs. Harrison said, her eyes twinkling with a mix of pride and curiosity. "So, what's next for you?"

"Berkeley," Lena replied. "I'll be studying cultural anthropology. I... I think it's the right choice."

Mrs. Harrison nodded thoughtfully. "Anthropology suits you. You've always been drawn to the stories of people, of civilizations. And if I know you, you won't stop at just studying them. You're chasing something bigger, aren't you?"

Lena hesitated, her gaze dropping to the floor. "It's the dreams," she admitted softly. "The crystal clock. It's still there, every night. I feel like it's connected to something ancient, something important. I need to understand it."

Mrs. Harrison's expression didn't waver. If anything, her smile deepened. "The questions you're asking, Lena, they're the kind that lead to discoveries—big ones. But remember, answers don't come all at once. They're fragments, pieces of a puzzle you'll spend your life putting together."

Lena felt a lump rise in her throat. Mrs. Harrison always had a way of making her feel seen, of validating her strange, unexplainable quest. "Thank you," she whispered. "For everything. You've helped me more than you know."

Mrs. Harrison reached out, squeezing Lena's hand gently. "The world needs people like you, Lena. People who see the connections others don't. Keep following that hum inside you. It'll lead you where you need to go."

Mrs. Harrison reached into her purse. She pulled out a small pouch and gave it to Lena.

Lena could see tears building in Mrs. Harrisons eyes. She said, "Lena, this belonged to my father since he was a young boy. It is a Crystal Talisman that he always wore or kept in his pocket."

"My father used to say it connects him to his search of time. I never knew what he meant, but since I met you and I can see your quest for knowledge, I want you to have the Talisman to remember me by."

Lena felt humbled that Mrs. Harrison would give such a gift to her, especially since it was a memory of her father. Lena gave Mrs. Harrison a hug and said, "Thank you. I will cherish the gift you have given me."

The sun was beginning to set as Lena walked out of the school building for the last time. The sky was painted in hues of orange and pink, and the warm breeze carried the scent of summer—a mix of freshly cut grass and blooming flowers.

Her phone buzzed in her pocket, a text from her mom: *Don't forget to come home for cake! We're celebrating YOU tonight!*

Lena smiled, tucking the phone away. She appreciated her mother's unwavering support, but she knew she needed a moment alone before rejoining the festivities. She wandered to the edge of the school grounds, finding a quiet spot beneath an old oak tree.

Sitting down, Lena let herself sink into the stillness. The hum in her chest was stronger now, a steady rhythm that felt like a second heartbeat. She closed her eyes and let the sensation wash over her, her mind drifting to the clock.

In her imagination, she saw the cave again, its walls shimmering with light. The symbols etched into the crystals seemed to shift and pulse, as if alive. And there, at the center, stood the clock, glowing faintly, its presence both serene and commanding.

The voice from her dream returned, faint but clear: *You are the chosen one. Protect the clock. Protect time. The balance must remain undisturbed.*

Lena opened her eyes, her breath coming in steady, measured beats. The hum was still there, vibrating softly in her chest. It wasn't just a dream. It never had been. The clock was real, and it was calling her. She didn't know how, or when, but she would find it. She had to.

That night, as the celebration wound down and the house grew quiet, Lena sat at her desk, staring at her notebook. Pages filled with sketches, notes, and fragments of theories stared back at her. She picked up her pen and wrote at the top of a blank page:

What comes next?

Beneath it, she scribbled a list of questions that had haunted her for years:

- Who created the clock?
- Why can I feel its hum?
- What does it mean to "protect time"?
- How do I find it?

Lena stared at the page for a long moment, her thoughts racing. The answers weren't here—not yet. But she was closer than she had ever been. The dreams, the hum, her studies—they were all leading her somewhere.

And she was ready to follow.

Graduation was the end of one chapter, but it was also the beginning of another. The world was waiting, and somewhere out there, the clock was too.

Chapter 7: The Vision of Peru

Lena's arrival at the University of California, Berkeley, had been a whirlwind of new faces, towering libraries, and the relentless buzz of intellectual curiosity. She threw herself into her studies with a fervor that surprised even her. Cultural Anthropology wasn't just a degree for Lena; it was a lens through which she could explore the ancient mysteries that had haunted her dreams for years. Each lecture about ancient civilizations, every late night spent poring over texts on energy rituals and forgotten rituals, brought her a little closer to understanding her connection to the crystal clock.

Her professors noticed her passion, especially Dr. Elena Vargas, an archaeologist renowned for her ground-breaking work on sacred geometry and ancient energy fields. Dr. Vargas quickly became a mentor to Lena, intrigued by her almost intuitive grasp of complex anthropological concepts. Lena's ability to interpret symbols and patterns from cultures spanning millennia was unparalleled among her peers. She often found herself staying after class, asking questions about obscure civilizations and their beliefs in time as a cyclical force rather than a linear one.

By the time Lena was finishing her final year, her reputation as a dedicated and insightful researcher had spread through the department. It was no surprise when Dr. Vargas approached her with an opportunity that would change her life. "There's a research team heading to Peru," Dr. Vargas had said, her tone both casual and charged with excitement. "They're investigating the Nazca Lines and potential energy anomalies in the Andes. I thought of you immediately. Your work with symbols and energy patterns could be invaluable to them." Lena had accepted without hesitation, knowing that this was no coincidence. It felt as though her entire academic journey had been building to this moment.

Graduating at the top of her class, Lena left Berkeley with more than a diploma; she carried the weight of her education, her newfound confidence, and a sense of purpose. The invitation to Peru wasn't just an academic opportunity—it was the next step in a journey that had begun long before her first day at Berkeley. It was as if the universe itself had conspired to guide her here, preparing her for a role far greater than she could have imagined.

Her mother had been both proud and concerned when Lena told her about the opportunity. "You've always been drawn to things most people don't see," she'd said. "Just… promise me you'll be careful, Lena. Whatever it is you're chasing, make sure it's worth the risk."
Lena was the envy of many well-wishers in her class. This was the opportunity of a life time and it was days away.

Commercial Flights took Lena and the rest of the research crew to Cusco. From there, they were off to Aguas Caliente on a small chartered flight.

Lena clutched her bag tightly and climbed aboard and took hers seat on the chartered plane. Its engines roared to life and they were on their way to Aguas Calientes, the gateway town near Machu Picchu. The interior was cramped, the rows of seats pressed so closely together that her knees brushed the back of the seat in front of her. She didn't mind. She stared out the window, her thoughts miles ahead of her, lost in the mountains and the mysteries they held.

The hum started again. Faint at first, like a whisper at the edge of her consciousness. It wasn't the noise of the engines or the vibrations of the plane. No, this hum came from within her, resonating deep in her chest, she hadn't felt this for a long time now. It was the frequency she had learned to associate with the crystal clock. She closed her eyes and leaned back against the headrest, allowing the rhythm of the plane's ascent to lull her into a meditative state.

The vision came to her suddenly.

Lena stood in the heart of a cavern, surrounded by walls that shimmered with countless crystals, their surfaces refracting light into a kaleidoscope of colors. The air was charged with energy, alive and almost humming with it. In the center of the cavern, towering and majestic, stood the crystal clock. Its surface glowed softly, pulsating in sync with the hum that seemed to vibrate through Lena's very bones.

It was more vivid than any dream she'd had before. She could feel the cool air of the cave against her skin, smell the faint mineral tang of the crystals, and hear the low, resonant tone that filled the space.

She stepped closer to the clock, her breath catching in her throat. It was both familiar and alien, an artifact that felt older than the mountains themselves. Its surface was smooth, flawless, and alive with shifting patterns of light. She reached out, her fingers trembling, and the moment her skin touched the crystal, the world froze.

Time stopped.

The hum grew louder, enveloping her in a cocoon of sound and energy. Lena's senses heightened—she could see every detail of the crystal's surface, feel the faint vibrations running through her body, even hear the slow, steady rhythm of her heartbeat. She wasn't just touching the clock; she was merging with it, becoming one with the ancient energy it held.

"Find it."

The words echoed around her, soft but commanding. Lena turned, searching for the source of the voice, but there was no one else in the cave. The clock's vibrations intensified, and she felt a surge of something indescribable—power, connection, destiny. The energy coursing through her seemed to transcend her physical form, tying her to something far greater.

And then, as suddenly as it had begun, the vision dissolved.

Lena's eyes snapped open. The cramped plane cabin came back into focus, the hum of the engines filling her ears. She blinked rapidly, disoriented, her breathing shallow as she tried to ground herself. The vision had felt so real, so immediate. She could still feel the echo of the clock's pulse in her fingertips, the command ringing in her ears.

"Find it."

Her heart raced as the plane began its descent, the landscape of the Andes growing larger in the window beside her. The rugged peaks stretched endlessly, their snow-capped summits gleaming in the sunlight. Somewhere in those mountains, she was certain, was the answer she had been searching for. The crystal clock wasn't just a dream or a fragment of her imagination. It was real, and it was waiting for her.

The plane touched down with a gentle jolt, and Lena exhaled slowly, trying to calm the storm of emotions inside her. As the team disembarked, the thin mountain air hit her immediately, cool and sharp. She adjusted her bag and followed the others toward the small terminal, her eyes constantly scanning the horizon.

The Andes seemed to stretch on forever, their jagged ridges casting deep shadows over the valleys below. There was an energy here, a presence she couldn't ignore. It wasn't just the natural beauty of the landscape—it was something deeper, something ancient. Lena could feel it in the soles of her boots as she walked, in the faint vibration that seemed to hum through the air.

"Breathtaking, isn't it?" a voice said beside her. She turned to see Professor Ruiz, one of the lead researchers on the team. A tall man with kind eyes and a weathered face, Ruiz had spent decades studying the mysteries of the Andes. He smiled warmly at Lena, gesturing to the mountains around them.

Lena nodded, her voice quiet. "It feels… alive."

Ruiz chuckled. "That's one way to put it. The Andes have a way of making you feel small. They've been here for millions of years, watching civilizations rise and fall. If these mountains could talk, I wonder what they'd tell us."

Lena smiled faintly, but her thoughts were already drifting. She wasn't just here to study the past; she was here to uncover something that transcended it.

The group piled into a series of waiting jeeps, their gear stowed in the back. The drive to the base camp was long and winding, the dirt roads hugging the edges of steep cliffs. Lena stared out the window, watching the landscape change as they climbed higher into the mountains. Fields of wildflowers gave way to rocky outcrops, and the air grew colder with each mile.

At last, they arrived at the camp—a cluster of canvas tents set against the backdrop of a towering peak. The researchers wasted no time unloading their equipment, their movements practiced and efficient. Lena, however, stood frozen, her eyes fixed on the horizon. The hum in her chest was stronger now, almost insistent.

"Lena?" Ruiz's voice broke through her thoughts. "Everything alright?"

She nodded quickly, shaking off the daze. "Yeah. Just… taking it all in."

Ruiz studied her for a moment, then gave a knowing smile. "You'll get used to it. The mountains have a way of getting under your skin. Let me know if you need anything."

As he walked away, Lena turned back to the horizon, her gaze lingering on the distant peaks. The hum thrummed steadily, a quiet reminder of her purpose.

That night, as the camp settled into a quiet rhythm, Lena sat alone outside her tent, staring up at the stars. The sky here was unlike anything she had ever seen—vast and infinite, with constellations that seemed close enough to touch. The Andes loomed around her, silent and watchful, their shadows stretching long in the moonlight.

She closed her eyes and let the stillness wash over her. The vision from the plane replayed in her mind, the words echoing once more: *Find it.*

The path was finally clear. Somewhere in these mountains, hidden among the ancient stones and forgotten ruins, was the crystal clock. And Lena was ready to find it.

For the first time in her life, she was feeling certain of her place in the world. The answers were within reach, waiting to be uncovered. All she had to do was follow the hum.

Chapter 8: The Hidden Temple

Today's exploration and research was going to take the research team on a trek into some rugged mountainous jungle terrain to study and find the source of elevated frequency noise in the area.

The sun dipped behind the jagged peaks of the Andes, casting the narrow mountain path into a cloak of shadow. Lena's breath came in short, shallow gasps as her team pressed forward. The air was thin, sharp, and cold at this altitude, but the discomfort was nothing compared to the burning anticipation that drove her forward. Each step brought her closer to the destination they had been seeking for days: the hidden temple, buried deep in these mountains.

And perhaps, within it, the crystal clock.

Lena's heart raced, though not just from exertion. The hum in her chest—the strange hum she had felt all her life—was stronger now, resonating through her bones with a clarity that made her skin tingle. She had dreamed of this moment, felt its inevitability since she first learned to name the dream. Now, it was as though the mountains themselves whispered promises of answers.

Behind her, Professor Ruiz led the team with quiet determination, his sharp eyes scanning the landscape. The others—archaeologists, anthropologists, and local guides—were equally focused, though their excitement was tempered by the weight of the journey. Lena could feel the mix of camaraderie and unease among them. They were all professionals, but this discovery felt different. The air here was alive, charged with an unspoken tension that no one could name.

The symbols had guided them here.

For weeks, they had studied the markings left behind on stones scattered throughout the region. Some were etched into massive boulders at sacred sites, others carved delicately into pottery fragments unearthed in nearby ruins. At first, the glyphs were an enigma, but slowly, a pattern emerged. Lena had spent sleepless nights poring over photos and sketches, comparing them to the ones in her dreams. When they finally uncovered a map—a crude but unmistakable representation of the mountain range.

Lena felt her heartbeat quicken—not from the altitude, but from the sense that something profound was about to happen.

The warmth in her pocket drew her attention. At first, she thought it was the heat of the day or perhaps her imagination playing tricks on her. But as the sensation grew stronger, she paused mid-step. Her hand instinctively reached into her jacket pocket, her fingers brushing against the smooth surface of the talisman.

Pulling it out, she was startled by what she saw. The talisman, which had always felt inert in her hands, now emitted a faint, otherworldly glow. Its surface was warm—not unpleasant, but comforting, like the touch of sunlight filtered through glass. Patterns she hadn't noticed before seemed to shimmer faintly under the glow, intricate designs that mirrored some of the symbols she had sketched in her notebook.

Lena stopped walking, staring at it in wonder. The research team, laden with equipment and focused on the path ahead, barely noticed her hesitation. She turned the talisman over in her hand, watching as the light pulsed faintly, almost in rhythm with the hum in her chest.

One of the researchers, a young geologist named Carlos, noticed her lingering behind. "Everything okay, Lena?" he asked, his voice tinged with concern.

She hesitated before answering, unsure how to explain what she was experiencing. "Yeah, I'm fine," she said, slipping the talisman back into her pocket. The warmth seemed to intensify briefly, as if acknowledging her action. "Just needed a second."

Carlos nodded and motioned toward the team ahead. "We're almost to the site. You don't want to miss this."

Lena nodded, falling back into step with the group. But her mind was racing. The talisman had never reacted like this before. What was it about this place—this moment—that was waking it up? The glow and warmth weren't random. They were tied to something here, something she was meant to be discovered.

As they continued their climb, the hum in her chest grew stronger, resonating in perfect harmony with the talisman. She didn't need to understand it fully to know one thing for certain: the talisman was guiding her, just as the voice in her dream had said it would.

"The path begins where the sun meets the stone," the voice had whispered. And now, with every step she took, Lena felt closer to unraveling the meaning of those words. The answers she had sought for so long were waiting, just beyond the next ridge.

Now, as they stood before a towering rock formation, their journey felt as though it had led them not just to a place, but to a moment of destiny.

"Here," Professor Ruiz said, pointing to a narrow crevice between two colossal boulders. His voice was hushed, as if the mountains themselves demanded reverence. "This is where the map leads."

Lena stepped forward, her gaze tracing the crevice's jagged edges. The faint markings etched into the stone confirmed it. These were the same symbols she had seen in her dreams—the same language of time and energy. The realization sent a chill through her, but it wasn't fear. It was certainty.

Professor Ruiz ran his hand across the rock etchings. After a moment of fumbling, there was a faint click, and a section of the stone slid aside, revealing a dark passage. He must have touched a mechanism that opened a passage into a cave. A rush of cold air escaped, carrying the scent of damp earth and something metallic, ancient. The air felt alive, almost breathing.

Collectively, the team decided and agreed they were going in to the cave. Each of them prepared a torch they carried with them. One by one they entered. Lena tightened the straps of her pack and stepped inside, her torch illuminating the passageway. The walls were lined with intricate carvings, symbols layered upon symbols, creating a story that felt older than memory itself. The air grew colder the deeper they went, and the hum in Lena's chest intensified, vibrating in harmony with the walls around her.

The narrow corridor widened into a vast chamber, and the sight that greeted them left the entire team in stunned silence.

The cave was enormous, its ceiling vanishing into the shadows above. The walls were lined with towering crystals, their surfaces gleaming faintly in the light of their torches. The chamber was so silent, so still, that Lena could hear her own heartbeat pounding in her ears.

And there it was.

At the far end of the chamber, standing like a sentinel, was the crystal clock. It was massive. Lena estimated it to be at least twenty feet tall and had at least a five foot diameter.

It was nothing like the fragile object she had imagined in her dreams. The clock was a towering structure of crystalline facets that seemed to shift and shimmer, even in the still air. Its surface was impossibly smooth, reflecting light in ways that defied explanation. Deep within its core, a pulsating glow throbbed rhythmically, as though the crystal itself were alive.

Lena's breath caught in her throat. This was it. The source of her dreams, the artifact she had spent her life chasing. It was real, and it was more magnificent than she could have ever imagined.

She stepped forward, her footsteps echoing in the vast chamber. Her heart pounded, the hum in her chest resonating with the crystal's pulse. It was calling to her, urging her closer.

"Lena," Professor Ruiz said, his voice a mix of awe and disbelief. "This… this is incredible. I've never seen anything like it."

The rest of the team murmured their agreement, their torches casting flickering light across the room. But Lena barely heard them. She was transfixed, her entire being drawn toward the crystal. The symbols carved into its base seemed to glow faintly, their meaning tantalizingly close to her grasp.

As if in a trance, she reached out her hand. The moment her fingers brushed the surface, a surge of energy shot through her, overwhelming and all-consuming. The room blurred, and suddenly Lena was somewhere else.

The vision was like a dream, yet sharper, clearer.

She stood in the same chamber, but it was alive with motion and light. Figures moved around her, their faces obscured but their purpose clear. These were ancient guardians, tending to the crystal with reverence. She watched as they performed rituals, their voices raised in harmonic chants that resonated with the crystal's hum.

The scene shifted, and Lena saw civilizations rise and fall. The crystal stood as a silent witness to the passage of time, its power a safeguard against forces that sought to exploit it. She felt the weight of its purpose, the immense responsibility it carried.

Then the vision darkened.

She saw figures cloaked in shadow, their hands grasping for the crystal with greedy intent. The air grew heavy, and Lena watched in horror as the crystal's glow dimmed, its energy faltering. The cave crumbled around it, and the delicate balance it had maintained began to unravel. Time itself fractured, the world dissolving into chaos.

A voice, ancient and commanding, echoed through the vision: *"Protect the clock. The balance must not be broken."*

The words reverberated through Lena's mind as the vision faded.

Her eyes snapped open, and she staggered backward, her hand slipping from the crystal's surface. Her chest heaved as she struggled to process what she had seen. The crystal wasn't just a relic. It was a guardian, a keystone in the fabric of time itself. And it was in danger.

"Lena?" Professor Ruiz's voice broke through her daze. "Are you alright?"

Before she could answer, the sound of footsteps echoed through the chamber.

The Team was barely able to appreciate the beauty of the Crystal in front of them.

Lena froze, her instincts screaming danger. The footsteps grew louder, heavier, and then she saw them—figures emerging from the shadows at the entrance.

The leader was a tall man cloaked in dark robes, his face partially hidden by a hood. His eyes burned with an intensity that sent a shiver down Lena's spine. Behind him, two others followed, their movements calculated, predatory.

"You shouldn't be here," the leader said, his voice low and menacing. "This temple is not yours to enter."

Lena's body tensed as the man's gaze fell on the crystal. There was no mistaking his intent. He had come for its power.

"Who are you?" Professor Ruiz demanded, stepping forward. "This is a protected archaeological site. You have no authority here."

Lena's voice cut through the oppressive tension. "You don't understand what you're dealing with," she said, her tone steady despite the fear coursing through her. "The crystal isn't a tool for power—it's a force of balance. If you try to use it, you'll destroy yourselves and everything around you." She took a step closer, her fingers still wrapped tightly around the talisman. It seemed to hum in response to her determination, resonating with the energy of the crystal.

The leader of the intruders sneered, his eyes flickering with cold amusement. "You think your resolve matters here? This is beyond balance, beyond your understanding. Time is ours to command." He raised his hand, and the two men flanking him stepped forward, their movements unnaturally swift. Lena could feel the distortion in the air, the faint ripple of energy emanating from the crystal as their intentions grew more hostile. The chamber seemed to shift, the edges of reality warping under the strain of their presence.

Summoning every ounce of courage, Lena closed her eyes and focused on the talisman in her hand. The vision from her dream surged back to her—the crystal pulsing, time bending around her, and the voice urging her to protect it. As the intruders moved closer, she felt the talisman connect with the energy of the crystal, the hum growing into a deep vibration that seemed to fill the entire chamber. With a sharp burst of light, the energy lashed out, creating a ripple that forced the intruders to falter. Their smug confidence gave way to confusion as the crystal's power surged against their presence, throwing them back.

Ruiz gasped, pulling Lena out of her focus. The intruders scrambled to regain their footing, but the leader raised his hand, signaling retreat. His cold, calculating eyes locked with Lena's for a long moment, and then he gave a small nod—an acknowledgment of her strength, but also a silent promise. "This isn't over," he said, his voice low and dangerous. *"You're not the only one chosen."* The three figures dissolved into the shadows, leaving the chamber eerily still. The hum of the crystal quieted, and Lena exhaled sharply, her heart pounding as she realized what had just transpired. For now, the crystal was safe. But the battle was far from over.

Chapter 9: Allies and Enemies

The team made a hasty exit from the cave or what the intruders had called a temple. As the last of them exited, the entrance to the cave closed without prompting. It left everyone in awe and surprise.

The trek back to camp was steeped in silence, save for the crunch of boots on gravel and the occasional snap of a twig underfoot. The air, heavy with tension, seemed to press against Lena's skin. The shadows stretched long under the moonlight, and the crystal's hum still reverberated faintly in her chest, as though it had imprinted itself permanently on her.

She glanced at Professor Ruiz, walking just ahead of her. His usual confidence was gone, replaced by a pensive silence. The rest of the team followed close behind, their expressions a mixture of exhaustion and unease. The hooded man's parting words echoed in her mind: *"You're not the only one chosen."*

The thought chilled her. Who were these others? And why had the crystal chosen her at all?

As they approached the perimeter of the camp, a sense of temporary relief washed over her. The familiar sight of tents, supply crates, and the faint glow of lanterns gave her a semblance of safety. But even here, under the stars, surrounded by her team, Lena couldn't shake the feeling that danger was only a heartbeat away.

The team gathered around the central firepit, its flickering light casting wavering shadows on their faces. The conversation was subdued at first—brief murmurs about the cave, the crystal, and the ominous visitors they had encountered. But the longer they sat, the more the tension began to boil over.

"We can't just abandon it there," one of the younger archaeologists, Sophie, said, her voice trembling with a mixture of fear and awe. "The crystal—it's too important. We need to study it. We could learn so much!"

"And risk being hunted by whoever those men were?" snapped Miguel, one of the guides. "They didn't look like they came for academic research. They looked like they came to kill anyone who stood in their way."

The group erupted into a cacophony of arguments, their voices growing louder as fear and ambition clashed.

"It's not just about them," Sophie countered, her voice rising. "This is a discovery that could change everything we know about history! We can't just walk away!"

"Enough!" Professor Ruiz's sharp tone cut through the noise. The group fell silent, their gazes turning toward him. His face was lined with exhaustion, but his eyes burned with determination. "We're dealing with forces we don't fully understand. Until we know more, our priority is safety. We document what we've found, and we alert the proper authorities. No one touches that crystal again until we have a plan."

His words brought a semblance of order to the group, but Lena could see the seeds of dissent growing in their expressions. Sophie's eyes lingered on the professor for a moment too long, her lips pressed into a thin line. Miguel and the other guides exchanged uneasy glances.

But Lena's attention was elsewhere. The hum in her chest had grown stronger again, and with it came a faint, nagging sense of unease. She scanned the edges of the camp, her eyes darting between the shadows. Something didn't feel right.

And then she saw it.

A figure moved just beyond the glow of the firelight, slipping between the trees with deliberate, silent steps. Her heart leapt into her throat.

"We're not alone," she whispered, her voice barely audible.

Miguel, who had been sitting closest to her, followed her gaze. His hand instinctively went to the knife at his belt. "What did you see?" he asked in a low voice.

"Someone's out there," Lena said, her pulse quickening.

Before she could say more, a faint rustle echoed through the trees, followed by the snap of a branch. The group froze, their eyes wide as they stared into the darkness.

"Who's there?" Professor Ruiz called, his voice steady but laced with tension.

For a moment, there was no response. And then, from the shadows, a voice emerged—low, calm, and eerily familiar.

"No need for alarm," the hooded man said, stepping into the firelight. His dark robe seemed to absorb the glow, making him appear as though he were part of the shadows themselves.

Lena shot to her feet, her hand instinctively clutching her talisman. The man's companions were close behind him, their expressions cold and unreadable.

"You again," Lena said, her voice sharper than she intended. "What do you want?"

The man smiled, a slow, calculated smile that didn't reach his eyes. "What I want is irrelevant. The question is, what do *you* want? Why are you here, chasing something you don't even understand?"

Lena's jaw tightened. She could feel the crystal's hum growing stronger, as if it were responding to the man's presence. "That's none of your business," she said firmly.

"On the contrary," he replied, his tone almost condescending. "You and I are more alike than you realize. The crystal has called to us both. The difference is, I understand its power. You... you're fumbling in the dark, hoping to stumble upon answers."

Lena's fingers curled into fists. "And what do you plan to do with that power? Use it for yourself? Manipulate time?"

The man's smile widened, his eyes gleaming with something that made Lena's stomach twist. "Time is not something to be manipulated. It's something to be mastered."

"You don't sound like someone who should have that kind of mastery," Miguel interjected, his knife glinting in the firelight.

The hooded man's gaze flicked to Miguel, his expression unbothered. "And you sound like someone who doesn't understand what's at stake. The crystal is not just an artifact. It's a key. A bridge. And if it falls into the wrong hands…"

He let the sentence hang, the implication heavy in the air.

"And you're the *right* hands?" Lena challenged, her voice rising.

The man tilted his head, studying her. For a moment, the firelight reflected something strange in his eyes—something that didn't feel entirely human. "Perhaps. Or perhaps not. But one thing is certain: if you and your little group meddle with forces beyond your comprehension, the consequences will be catastrophic."

The silence that followed was suffocating.

"Leave," Professor Ruiz said finally, his voice low but firm. "You're trespassing on our camp. We've already reported this site to the authorities. You have no claim here."

The hooded man's expression darkened, his smile vanishing. He took a step closer, his presence towering. "Do you think the authorities can protect you? Do you think they'll even begin to understand what you've found?"

He turned his gaze back to Lena, his eyes piercing. "The crystal has chosen you, hasn't it? You feel it, don't you? The pull. The hum. The way it calls to you. It's not just an artifact to you. It's part of you."

Lena's breath hitched, but she refused to let him see her uncertainty. "I don't know what you're talking about."

The man chuckled softly. "You will. Soon enough."

And with that, he turned and melted back into the shadows, his companions following silently behind him.

The camp erupted into frantic whispers the moment the intruders were gone.

"Who the hell was that?" Sophie demanded, her voice shaking.

"They're not archaeologists," Miguel muttered darkly. "That much is obvious."

Lena said nothing. Her mind was racing, replaying the man's words over and over. He knew about the crystal, about the way it called to her. And he was right—she *did* feel it. The connection, the pull. But what did it mean?

As the night wore on, the tension in the camp didn't abate. No one would sleep, their eyes constantly scanning the shadows for any sign of movement. Lena sat by the fire, clutching her talisman and staring into the flames.

The crystal was more than she had imagined. More than any of them had imagined.

And if what the man had said was true, she wasn't the only one who sought its power.

She was surrounded by allies and enemies—but in the growing chaos, she wasn't sure which was which.

Chapter 10: The Shaman's Wisdom

Lena was feeling the stress and tension of her team. The hooded man they had encountered earlier that day—a mysterious figure who seemed to appear out of nowhere and vanish just as quickly—had left everyone uneasy. Whispers among her teammates about curses, myths, and bad omens only fueled the tension. Lena, however, wasn't easily shaken. She felt something beyond fear: an unrelenting pull, a hum in her chest that had only grown stronger since arriving at Machu Picchu. That hum guided her now as she decided to take a walk into the small village near their camp, needing solitude to process the day's events.

The village was alive with activity despite the late hour. Vendors were packing up their stalls, children were chasing each other through narrow cobblestone streets, and the faint sound of pan flutes drifted through the cool evening air. Lena wandered aimlessly, her mind preoccupied with the glowing talisman in her pocket and the symbols she had uncovered. She felt the weight of responsibility pressing down on her—questions of why she had been chosen, what the clock wanted from her, and how she was supposed to protect it. Lost in thought, she almost didn't notice the elderly man standing in the shadows of a dimly lit corner, watching her.

The man was draped in a long, woven shawl adorned with intricate patterns that seemed to shimmer faintly in the moonlight. His eyes, piercing and impossibly dark, held a wisdom that unnerved Lena. For a moment, she hesitated, but then the hum in her chest flared, urging her forward. As if sensing her hesitation, the man tilted his head and gestured for her to approach. Something about him felt familiar, as though he had stepped out of the dreams that had haunted her for years.

"You carry something ancient," he said in a low, gravelly voice as she stepped closer. His gaze flicked briefly to her pocket, and

Lena's fingers instinctively tightened around the talisman. "Do you know what it is you hold?"

Lena hesitated, unsure how much to reveal. "It's… important," she said cautiously. "I think it's connected to something—something bigger than me."

The man smiled faintly, a gesture that was neither reassuring nor threatening. "That 'something bigger' has been waiting for you," he said, his voice carrying the weight of certainty. "But it comes with a price. You cannot carry its power without understanding its burden."

Lena's breath caught in her throat. She wanted to ask what he meant, but before she could speak, the man turned and began walking down a narrow path that led away from the main street. He paused, glancing over his shoulder. "If you seek answers, follow me."

Every instinct in Lena screamed caution, but the hum in her chest roared with urgency, overpowering her fear. She followed him, weaving through the darkened alleys until they emerged on the outskirts of the village. There, nestled beneath an ancient, gnarled tree, was a small stone hut. Smoke wafted gently from its chimney, carrying the scent of burning herbs.

Inside, the hut was dimly lit by flickering candles. The walls were lined with shelves crammed with jars, bundles of dried plants, and strange trinkets. In the center of the room, the man motioned for Lena to sit on a low stool. He knelt across from her, retrieving a small bowl filled with dark liquid and setting it between them.

"The talisman you carry is not just a key—it is a bridge," he said, his voice low and resonant. "It connects you to the flow of time and the ancient guardians who came before you. But to unlock its full power, you must prove yourself worthy."

Lena frowned, gripping the talisman tightly. "How? What do I have to do?"

The shaman didn't answer immediately. Instead, he dipped his fingers into the bowl of dark liquid and traced a symbol onto her palm—a symbol she recognized from the walls of the crystal cave in her dreams. The moment his finger touched her skin, the hum in her chest intensified, reverberating through her entire body. Images flooded her mind: the crystal clock, the glowing cave, the balance teetering on the edge of chaos.

"You must walk the path that lies before you," the shaman said, his voice a distant echo in her ears. "Trust the the sound you hear within you. It will guide you to what you seek. But beware— your journey will test your heart, your mind, and your soul. Your training is beginning."

With the bewildering comment, the Shaman ask Lena to present her crystal for him to see. Reluctantly Lena did this. The Shaman gazed at it and produced an identical crystal to Lena. "Two must become one," the Shaman said. "Hold the two together."

As Lena accepted the half crystal from the Shaman. In the dim light, she looked closely at the two Crystals. When she held them together, the two crystals seeming fused together. They were now one.

"When you are not with the Crystal in the cave, the Talisman will allow you to always be part of the Crystal. Your thoughts will transmit and change to reality."

There was so much information that the Shaman was giving her.

Lena found herself trembling, her palm tingling where the symbol had been drawn. The shaman's eyes bore into hers, filled with both warning and compassion. "The choice is yours, child," he said. "But remember this: power without wisdom is destruction. And the balance must never be disturbed."

Lena nodded, her resolve hardening. She didn't fully understand what lay ahead, but she knew one thing: the path had chosen her, and she wouldn't turn away.

The evening air in the village grew cooler as Lena walked back to her team's camp, her thoughts heavy with the Shaman's words. The pendant in her hand seemed to radiate a quiet warmth, as if it were alive, pulsing in rhythm with her heartbeat. She held it tightly, letting the steady hum reassure her as she moved through the dimly lit paths of the village.

The Shaman's words echoed in her mind: *"You are part of this balance, just as the crystal is."*

For years, Lena had felt the call of the Crystal Clock in her dreams, its hum resonating within her. But this was the first time someone had confirmed what she had always feared and hoped—that it wasn't just a dream, that she wasn't imagining the connection. She had been chosen, but the weight of that responsibility was overwhelming.

As she approached the camp, Lena's steps slowed. She could hear the low murmurs of her team gathered around the central fire. The flames cast flickering shadows on their faces, reflecting their exhaustion and the tension of the past days.

When she stepped into the circle of firelight, all eyes turned to her. Professor Ruiz stood, his expression a mixture of relief and curiosity. "Lena, where have you been? We were starting to worry."

"I needed some air," Lena said, her voice steady. She slid the pendant into her pocket, deciding not to mention the Shaman just yet. She wasn't ready to explain what had just happened—not until she had time to process it herself.

Ruiz studied her for a moment before nodding. "We've been talking about what to do next. Those men—whoever they were—they're not going to stop. And if they know about the crystal…" He trailed off, his meaning clear.

Lena sat down by the fire, her fingers brushing against the pendant in her pocket. She wanted to tell them about the Shaman, about the wisdom he had shared, but she wasn't sure how they would react. Would they believe her? Or would they dismiss it as superstition?

Miguel, one of the guides, broke the silence. "We should leave. Now. There's nothing here worth risking our lives over."

"Nothing?" Sophie, the young archaeologist, snapped. "That crystal could be the discovery of the century! We can't just abandon it!"

"And what happens if those men come back?" Miguel shot back. "Do you think they'll let us leave alive if we get in their way?"

The group fell into tense silence. Lena listened, her mind racing. They were all missing the bigger picture. The crystal wasn't just a scientific discovery or a potential threat—it was the key to something far greater. And if it fell into the wrong hands…

Lena's grip tightened around the pendant. She had to speak up.

"We can't let them take control of it," she said firmly, her voice cutting through the quiet. "The crystal isn't just a relic or a tool.

It's… something more. Something powerful. If those men get their hands on it, they could destroy everything."

Her words hung in the air, the weight of them pressing down on the group.

"What are you saying, Lena?" Sophie asked, her tone skeptical. "That the crystal can really stop time? That it's some kind of magic artifact?"

Lena hesitated. How could she explain what the Shaman had told her without sounding insane? But then she remembered his final words: *"Trust in yourself and the guidance you have received."*

"I don't know exactly what it is," Lena admitted, her gaze steady. "But I know it's dangerous in the wrong hands. And I know that it's connected to me. I've felt it calling me, even before we came to Peru. This isn't just about research or discovery. It's about protecting something that shouldn't be used for power or control."

Professor Ruiz frowned, his expression thoughtful. "You're suggesting we protect it? How? Those men—whoever they are—are clearly organized. Armed. They'll stop at nothing to get what they want. I say we should tell the authorities and get out of here."

"We don't need to fight them," Lena said. "We just need to ensure the crystal stays out of their reach. We can document what we've found, share it with the right people, and then…" She paused, her mind racing. "Then we make sure the crystal is safe, hidden, where no one can use it for harm."

Sophie looked skeptical, but Miguel seemed to consider her words. "And what makes you so sure you can protect it?"

Lena met his gaze, her hand still clutching the pendant. "Because I'm not doing this alone."

The group exchanged uneasy glances, but no one argued further. The tension around the fire remained thick, but the conversation shifted to logistics—how to secure their findings, they can't relocate it, and how to avoid another confrontation with the hooded figures.

Later that night, Lena lay in her tent, staring up at the canvas ceiling. The pendant rested against her chest, its warmth soothing. She replayed the Shaman's words in her mind, searching for clarity.

"The power of the crystal lies not just in its physical form. It is a force of the universe itself, connected to every atom, every particle."

Her dreams that night were vivid, more vivid than they had been in weeks. She was back in the cave, standing before the Crystal Clock. The hum of the crystal filled the air, resonating with the rhythm of her heartbeat. But this time, the vision was different.

The clock was not still. It was moving, its inner mechanisms turning slowly, almost imperceptibly. And as Lena reached out to touch it, she saw the faint outline of the hooded man standing in the shadows, watching her.

"You cannot hide forever," his voice echoed, cold and distant.

Lena woke with a start, her heart pounding. The tent was dark, the camp silent except for the faint rustle of the wind. But the sense of urgency remained.

She knew now, more than ever, that the Shaman was right. The crystal's power was not something to be wielded lightly. It was a responsibility, a burden she had been chosen to bear and she had to be careful.

And as she lay there in the stillness of the night, one thought burned brighter than all the rest:

She would protect the crystal, no matter the cost.

Chapter 11: The First Revelation

The jungle seemed alive as Lena and her team made their way back to the cave. The rustling leaves, the buzzing of unseen insects, and the distant calls of birds formed a symphony that resonated with an ancient, almost sacred energy. The path was narrow and uneven, and every step felt as though it was pulling Lena closer to something monumental. She could feel the hum of the crystal growing stronger, vibrating deep within her chest as if it were a heartbeat separate from her own.

Her team, led by Professor Ruiz, walked in a tense silence. They all felt the weight of what lay ahead, though none of them could fully comprehend the pull Lena was experiencing. For them, this was already more than just another excavation, another historical artifact to study and document. For Lena, it was something far greater.

When they finally reached the cave, Professor Ruiz slid his hand across the etched markings outside the closed entrance in the same way he had the day before. The entrance to the cave opened and one by one, everyone stepped inside, the air grew heavier, charged with an energy that seemed to cling to their skin. The torches they carried flickered against the walls, illuminating the intricate carvings that lined the passageway— symbols and patterns that Lena now recognized from her dreams.

Once again the chamber opened up before them, and there it was.

The **Crystal Clock** stood at the heart of the room, a towering monolith pulsing faintly with its own light. It shimmered, its edges sharp and crystalline, its surface smooth and reflective. It was larger than Lena had imagined, an imposing figure of pure energy and light, radiating a presence that seemed to fill the entire chamber.

The rest of the team stopped in their tracks, staring in awe once again. Professor Ruiz was the first to speak, his voice hushed.

"I can't get over how beautiful it is. It's... magnificent," he said, his words almost a whisper.

But Lena's entire focus was on the crystal. The hum she had felt earlier was now a steady vibration, a rhythm that resonated in her very core. She stepped forward, her feet moving of their own accord.

"Careful, Lena," Professor Ruiz said, his tone cautious.

She barely heard him. Her hand reached out, her fingers trembling as they approached the crystal's surface. She felt the pull grow stronger with each step, the air around her thick and electric. When her fingers finally made contact, a shock of energy coursed through her, and the world around her changed.

Time stopped.

The air stilled. The flickering of the torches froze, their flames caught in mid-dance. Her teammates stood motionless, their expressions of awe and curiosity frozen in place. Even the faint sound of the jungle outside was gone, replaced by a profound silence.

Lena's breath caught in her throat as she looked around. She was moving, but everything else was suspended, locked in a moment that seemed to stretch infinitely. The crystal beneath her hand pulsed gently, its hum now a deep, resonant tone that filled her entire being.

She stepped away from the crystal, her movements slow and deliberate. The stillness was disorienting but also strangely calming. She felt as though she had stepped outside of reality itself, into a realm where time held no power.

Her gaze returned to the crystal, and as she stared into its shimmering depths, and as before, she saw something—images, fleeting but vivid. Ancient rituals performed in front of the crystal. Figures dressed in ceremonial robes, their hands raised as if channeling its energy. Wars fought, kingdoms rising and falling, all tied to the crystal's immense power.

Then she saw something else. A glimpse of the future. A world in chaos, torn apart by those who sought to control the crystal's power. The vision was brief but clear, and it left Lena with a deep sense of dread.

She blinked, and the images faded. Time resumed.

The torches flickered once more, their light casting shadows on the walls. The sounds of the jungle returned, faint but steady. Her teammates stirred, their movements jerky as if they had just woken from a deep sleep.

Professor Ruiz looked at her, his expression one of confusion and awe. "Lena, what just happened? It felt like... like something shifted."

"I touched it," Lena said, her voice steady but soft. "Time... stopped."

The words hung in the air, and for a moment, no one spoke.

"Stopped?" Sophie, one of the archaeologists, repeated, her voice tinged with disbelief. "What do you mean, stopped?"

Lena took a deep breath, trying to put the experience into words. "Everything froze. The torches, the sounds... even all of you. It was like the world itself paused, but I could still move.

And the crystal—it showed me things. Visions of the past. Of the future."

"Visions?" Professor Ruiz's brow furrowed.

"Rituals," Lena said, her voice growing more confident. "People using the crystal's power. Wars fought over it. And... destruction. If it falls into the wrong hands, it could destroy everything."

The team exchanged uneasy glances.

"Lena," Professor Ruiz said carefully, "are you saying the crystal has the power to stop time? To show the future?"

"Yes," Lena said without hesitation.

Professor Ruiz walk closer to the crystal, examining its surface in more detail. He reached out and touched the crystal, but nothing happened. "Why didn't everything stop when I touched the crystal?"

"It's not just an artifact. It's... alive. It's connected to time itself. And it's connected to me."

The room fell silent again as the weight of her words sank in.

That night, back at camp, Lena couldn't sleep. She sat by the fire, staring into the flames as the others rested in their tents. The joined Talisman that Mrs. Harrison and the Shaman had given her rested in her hand, its smooth surface warm to the touch.

She turned it over in her fingers, thinking about the visions she had seen. The Shaman's words echoed in her mind: *"The crystal will show you what you need to know, when you need to know it."*

The crystal had chosen her. She didn't fully understand why, but she couldn't deny the truth of it. She had felt its power, seen its potential. And she knew that she had a responsibility to protect it.

But how?

The hooded figures who had confronted them at the cave—they weren't just after the crystal for its historical significance. They knew its true power, and they wanted to control it. Lena's visions had made it clear what would happen if they succeeded.

She clenched the pendant tightly in her fist, determination hardening her resolve.

She would find a way to protect the crystal. She would learn to understand its power, to wield it if necessary.

The future depended on it.

The jungle was alive with the hum of nocturnal creatures, their calls weaving a symphony of the unknown. Lena lay on her cot in the corner of the temple chamber, staring up at the stone ceiling, her mind too restless for sleep. Ever since she had touched the Crystal Clock and felt its immense power ripple through her, an unshakable pull had anchored her thoughts to it. She had seen it—time, bending and freezing, a force malleable in her hands. And yet, she had barely scratched the surface of its potential.

The night air was heavy, the stillness of the team's camp punctuated only by the rhythmic sound of their breathing. Lena turned her head toward the faint glow of the crystal in the central chamber. Its presence was magnetic, drawing her toward it like the tide to the moon. Her fingers twitched, itching to feel its surface again, to see if she could replicate what had happened before—or push its power further.

She sat up slowly, careful not to wake anyone, and made her way to the crystal. Each step seemed to echo in the vast chamber, the quiet amplifying her racing thoughts. The eternal crystal torches mounted on the walls cast flickering shadows that danced across the crystal's surface. Standing before it, Lena hesitated. Her chest tightened as the memory of her previous experience washed over her—the hum in her chest, the frozen stillness of the world, and the overwhelming sense of control.

This time, she told herself, it wouldn't be an accident. She would test its limits deliberately, with precision.

Her palm hovered over the crystal's smooth, shimmering surface. The air around it vibrated faintly, a resonance that pulsed in time with her heartbeat. Closing her eyes, Lena pressed her hand to the crystal.

The hum intensified immediately, coursing through her body like a wave. Her breathing slowed, and the air thickened. The room seemed to blur at the edges, the boundaries of reality softening. A familiar stillness began to creep over her, the world shifting as time itself yielded to her will.

When she opened her eyes, everything had stopped. The flicker of torchlight hung frozen in mid-motion, the flames' gentle sway suspended as if captured in glass. The faint rustle of the jungle outside had vanished, leaving only silence.

Lena's breath hitched. She had done it again.

She took a step forward, marveling at the frozen world around her. The ground beneath her feet felt solid, but the air was thick, as if she were moving through water. Her movements created faint ripples in the stillness, a distortion that seemed to linger in her wake. She reached out toward Ruiz, her fingers brushing the edge of his sleeve. It was stiff, unyielding, like stone.

Time wasn't just stopped—it was crystallized.

Lena turned her attention back to the crystal. Its glow was brighter now, its hum louder, almost a song vibrating through the air. She closed her eyes again, focusing on the sensations coursing through her. The crystal wasn't just a tool; it was alive, pulsing with energy and intention. It was responding to her, amplifying her desires and bending reality to her will.

She took a deep breath and concentrated, thinking back to the day's events. She focused on one specific moment—Professor Ruiz's doubt, his hesitation that had stalled their progress. She visualized it clearly, imagining the scene unfolding differently. Ruiz trusting her instinctively, the team following her lead without question.

The crystal's hum deepened, and the air seemed to shift. Lena opened her eyes as a jolt of energy shot through her, the world snapping back into motion.

She staggered slightly, blinking as her surroundings came back into focus. The torches flickered as if nothing had happened. The jungle's symphony resumed, distant but steady. It was time for her to get back to the camp before the others would wake up.

The next morning as Lena exited her tent, Professor Ruiz was standing near the camp fire, his expression transformed. The doubt that had lingered in his eyes earlier was gone, replaced by awe. "This is incredible," he murmured, his voice reverent. "I don't know why I ever doubted you, Lena. This discovery—it's beyond anything I imagined."

The team had decided to move their camp to the cave. It had plenty of room and from there they would eliminate valuable time hiking back and forth to their camp by the village. The team managed to set up their camp site and their monitoring equipment. By then the day had come to an end.

The jungle was alive with the hum of nocturnal creatures, their calls weaving a symphony of the unknown. Lena lay on her cot in the corner of the temple chamber, staring up at the stone ceiling, her mind too restless for sleep. Ever since she had touched the Crystal Clock and felt its immense power ripple through her, an unshakable pull had anchored her thoughts to it. She had seen it—time, bending and freezing, a force malleable in her hands. And yet, she had barely scratched the surface of its potential.

The night air was heavy, the stillness of the team's camp punctuated only by the rhythmic sound of their breathing. Lena turned her head toward the faint glow of the crystal in the central chamber. Its presence was magnetic, drawing her toward it like the tide to the moon. Her fingers twitched, itching to feel its surface again, to see if she could replicate what had happened before—or push its power further.

She sat up slowly, careful not to wake anyone, and made her way to the crystal. Each step seemed to echo in the vast chamber, the quiet amplifying her racing thoughts. The eternal crystal torches mounted on the walls cast flickering shadows that danced across the crystal's surface. Standing before it, Lena hesitated. Her chest tightened as the memory of her previous experience washed over her—the hum in her chest, the frozen stillness of the world, and the overwhelming sense of control.

This time, she told herself, it wouldn't be an accident. She would test its limits deliberately, with precision.

Her palm hovered over the crystal's smooth, shimmering surface. The air around it vibrated faintly, a resonance that pulsed in time with her heartbeat. Closing her eyes, Lena pressed her hand to the crystal.

The hum intensified immediately, coursing through her body like a wave. Her breathing slowed, and the air thickened. The room seemed to blur at the edges, the boundaries of reality softening. A familiar stillness began to creep over her, the world shifting as time itself yielded to her will.

When she opened her eyes, everything had stopped. The flicker of torchlight hung frozen in mid-motion, the flames' gentle sway suspended as if captured in glass. The faint rustle of the jungle outside had vanished, leaving only silence.

Lena's breath hitched again. She had done it again.

Lena's stomach flipped. The scene was exactly as she had visualized it. She had rewritten the moment, bending the timeline to align with her desires. It worked.

But as the seconds ticked by, unease crept into her chest. The room felt... off. The air carried a faint charge, an unnatural weight. The torches' flames flickered erratically, their light casting distorted shadows on the walls. She glanced at the rest of the team. Their expressions were calm, even serene, but there was something unsettling in the way they moved—slightly too smooth, too synchronized, as if they were part of a choreographed performance.

A faint rustling at the chamber's entrance made her freeze. She turned, her heart pounding as the shadows shifted.

A figure emerged from the darkness, his silhouette sharp against the flickering light. It was the hooded man. His eyes gleamed with a cold, unnatural light, and his movements were deliberate, predatory. Two more figures followed, their faces obscured but their presence equally menacing.

"You felt it, didn't you?" the hooded man said, his voice low and resonant. "The shift."

Lena's breath caught in her throat. How had he gotten here? She hadn't sensed anyone following them. The man stepped closer, his gaze fixed on her with an intensity that made her skin crawl.

"You've barely scratched the surface of its power," he continued, nodding toward the crystal. "But even a novice like you can create ripples. Do you feel it? The instability? The imbalance? That's what happens when you tamper with forces you don't understand."

Lena clenched her fists, her fear giving way to anger. "What do you want?" she demanded.

The man smiled, cold and cruel. "The crystal doesn't belong to you. It was never yours to claim. You're playing with something far beyond your comprehension."

"She's done nothing wrong," Professor Ruiz interjected, stepping forward. "We're here to study and protect it."

The man's expression darkened. "Protect it? You've already disturbed its balance. The crystal isn't some artifact to be studied—it's a gateway, a key. And in the wrong hands, it can destroy everything."

The air in the chamber grew colder, the shadows deepening as the hooded man advanced. His companions flanked him, their presence heavy and oppressive. Lena's heart raced as she realized the gravity of the situation. This wasn't just about the crystal anymore. It was about power—control over time itself.

"Let us have access to it," the man said, his tone leaving no room for argument. "Or face the consequences."

Lena stepped in front of the crystal, her resolve hardening. "No," she said firmly. "I won't let you."

The man's smile faded, replaced by a steely glare. "You don't understand what you're dealing with, girl. The crystal has called to others before you—stronger, wiser, more prepared. And yet, they all failed. You will too."

Lena's grip tightened on the pendant given to her. Lena released her grip on the stoppage of time that she was experimenting with. The pendants warmth steadied her, its hum aligning with the crystal's resonance. She glanced at Ruiz, his face pale but determined, and then at the rest of the team. They didn't fully understand what was at stake, but they trusted her. She had to protect them.

The hooded man raised a hand, and the air seemed to crackle with energy. "This is your last chance," he said. "Surrender the crystal, or suffer the consequences."

Lena stood her ground, her pulse pounding in her ears. She could feel the crystal's energy surging behind her, its power flowing through her veins. She didn't know how, but she knew she had to fight.

And she wasn't going to back down.

The tension in the chamber was palpable, like the air itself was holding its breath. Lena's fingers curled tighter around the pendant, its warmth a reminder of the shaman's words: **Trust your connection to the crystal.** She could feel the power coursing through her, alive and responsive, as though it were waiting for her command.

The hooded man stepped forward, the energy around him almost palpable. His companions mirrored his movements, their silence more unsettling than words could ever be. The flickering torchlight danced across their shadowed faces, giving them an almost otherworldly appearance.

"You don't have to do this," Lena said, her voice steady despite the fear swirling inside her. "The crystal isn't meant to be controlled. It's a balance, a safeguard. If you try to control it—if you misuse it—you could destroy everything."

The man chuckled darkly. "Such noble words from someone who just bent time to her will." He gestured around the room, his gaze piercing. "You've already disturbed the balance, girl. Don't pretend you're innocent."

Lena's heart sank. He was right—she had tampered with the timeline, even if only slightly. The unease she felt now was a consequence of her actions, and it was a weight she wasn't sure she was prepared to bear. But she couldn't let him win. Whatever his intentions were, they weren't pure. The crystal had shown her that much.

"I can feel its instability," the man continued, his tone softer now, almost coaxing. "It's already slipping, isn't it? The fabric of time fraying at the edges. Give me access to the crystal, and I can fix it. I can restore the balance before it's too late."

Lena hesitated, doubt creeping into her mind. What if he was telling the truth? What if she was making things worse by holding onto the crystal? But then she remembered the vision—the future the crystal had shown her, where its power was exploited and time itself unraveled. This man wasn't here to protect the balance. He was here to seize control.

"No," Lena said firmly, planting her feet. "You're not touching it."

The man's smile faded, replaced by a cold, calculating glare. "So be it."

He raised his hand, and a surge of energy erupted from his palm, crackling like lightning as it shot toward Lena. She flinched, instinctively raising the pendant in front of her. The talisman pulsed with light, absorbing the energy and deflecting it back toward the man. The force of the impact sent him staggering, his companions moving quickly to steady him.

The crystal behind Lena glowed brighter, its hum rising to a deafening pitch. The room seemed to tremble, the walls vibrating with the intensity of its power. Lena felt it coursing through her, an unrelenting force that seemed to amplify her every thought, her every emotion.

The hooded man straightened, his expression twisting with anger. "You've barely begun to understand what you're dealing with," he growled. "But if you won't surrender, I'll take it by force."

He motioned to his companions, and they spread out, their movements deliberate and menacing. Lena's mind raced. She couldn't fight them on her own—not without fully understanding the crystal's power. But she couldn't let them take control of it either.

"Professor Ruiz!" she called, her voice cutting through the chaos. "Get the team out of here. Now!"

Ruiz hesitated, torn between his loyalty to the team and helping Lena and his fear of the escalating situation. But when the hooded man advanced again, Ruiz nodded, gathering the rest of the team and ushering them toward the exit. Lena could hear their hurried footsteps retreating down the corridor, but her focus remained on the intruders.

The man raised his hand again, another surge of energy building around him. Lena tightened her grip on the pendant, channeling the crystal's power as she prepared to defend herself. The hum grew louder, the air crackling with tension.

And then it happened.

The crystal erupted in a blinding flash of light, its energy spilling out in all directions. Lena felt herself lifted off the ground, her body weightless as the force enveloped her. Time seemed to fracture, the room splintering into shards of moments—past, present, and future overlapping in a chaotic swirl. She caught glimpses of the temple as it once was, filled with worshippers kneeling before the crystal. She saw herself as a child, standing in the doorway of her childhood home, the faint hum of the crystal echoing in the distance. And she saw a future—a future where the crystal lay shattered, its pieces scattered across a desolate landscape.

The vision was overwhelming, a flood of images and sensations that threatened to drown her. But amidst the chaos, Lena felt something else: clarity. The crystal wasn't just showing her the possibilities—it was guiding her, helping her understand its purpose.

As the light faded, Lena found herself back in the chamber, her feet firmly on the ground. The hooded man and his companions were disoriented, staggering as they tried to regain their balance. The crystal's glow had dimmed, but its presence was stronger than ever, a steady pulse that resonated through the room.

Lena's mind was clear now. She understood what she had to do.

"You don't belong here," she said, her voice calm but firm. "This crystal isn't yours to take. Leave now and never come back, or you'll regret it."

The man's gaze hardened, but there was a flicker of doubt in his eyes. He could feel the shift, the power that Lena had begun to harness. He knew he was outmatched.

"This isn't over," he snarled, backing away. "You've meddled with forces beyond your control. You'll see the consequences soon enough."

With that, he turned and disappeared into the shadows, his companions following close behind. The room fell silent, the tension slowly dissipating.

Lena exhaled, her shoulders sagging with relief. She turned to the crystal, its soft glow reassuring her that she had made the right choice. But she knew this was only the beginning. The man's warning echoed in her mind, a reminder of the challenges that lay ahead.

She would need to learn more—about the crystal, about herself, and about the forces that sought to control them both. But for now, she had succeeded. She had protected the crystal, and she had taken her first step toward mastering its power.

As she made her way out of the chamber, Lena felt a renewed sense of purpose. The journey was far from over, but she was ready for whatever came next. The crystal had chosen her for a reason, and she wouldn't let it down.

Chapter 13: The Chase

The air was saturated with the earthy scent of rain-soaked foliage, and Lena's every breath seemed to echo against the walls of the cave. The jungle outside was alive with the chatter of nocturnal creatures, but their sounds felt distant, overshadowed by the silence of the chamber and the crystal's relentless hum. She stood frozen, her fingers had lightly brushing the crystal's surface. Each touch sent ripples of energy through her body, anchoring her to the strange connection she was still learning to navigate.

The events of the past day lingered in her mind, a chaotic mix of revelations, warnings, and experiments. She had altered time itself, bent its flow in ways she couldn't yet comprehend, and though the consequences had seemed minimal at first, Lena couldn't shake the feeling that something—someone—was closing in. Every moment since had been tainted by a quiet paranoia, an anticipation of what might come next.

Her suspicions solidified when she heard it—a faint rustle, the unmistakable sound of boots scuffing against stone.

She froze, her senses heightened.

The noise wasn't a casual disturbance. It was deliberate, calculated. Someone was moving through the temple.

Lena stepped back, her hand falling away from the crystal. The hum in her chest quickened, her pulse pounding in response. She slipped into the shadows of the chamber, her body tense and ready. Peering out, she caught sight of two figures emerging from the temple's entrance, their forms silhouetted against the faint light of dawn.

They weren't part of her team.

Lena squinted, her stomach twisting. One of them was tall, muscular, with a weapon strapped to his side. The other moved with a precise, almost predatory grace, clutching something metallic in his gloved hand—a tool, perhaps, designed to breach the crystal's protective sanctity. Their movements were purposeful, their intent clear.

They weren't here to explore. They were here for the crystal. And, if they knew its secret, they might also be after her.

Lena's hand instinctively reached for the pendant hanging from her neck—the talisman the shaman had given her. It was warm against her skin, its energy pulsing faintly. She had hidden its significance from the team, afraid of what they might think. But these men—they knew. Somehow, they understood the connection between the talisman and the crystal, and they wouldn't stop until they had both.

Fear coursed through her veins, but Lena forced herself to stay calm. Panic wouldn't help her now. She needed a plan.

The men began moving deeper into the chamber, their eyes scanning the room. Lena slipped silently into a darkened corridor, her footsteps light against the stone floor. Her breathing was shallow, her ears straining to catch any sound of pursuit. She couldn't face them head-on—not without fully understanding the crystal's power—but she also couldn't let them use it. She needed time to think, to act.

The corridor twisted and turned, its walls narrowing as Lena moved deeper into the temple. She didn't dare slow down. The faint echoes of the men's voices followed her, growing louder with each passing second.

"Spread out," one of them ordered, his voice low but firm. "She couldn't have gone far."

Lena's heart raced. They were close—too close.

She pushed herself harder, her legs burning as she sprinted down the winding passage. The air grew cooler, heavier, as she descended further into the temple's depths. Her mind raced alongside her feet, searching for a way out, a way to turn the situation in her favor.

The passage finally opened into a large chamber, and Lena skidded to a halt, her eyes darting around the space. The walls were covered in intricate carvings, glowing faintly in the dim light. Ancient symbols spiraled across the stone, their meanings just out of reach. At the far end of the room, a massive stone door loomed, its surface etched with even more markings.

It was her only way out.

Lena rushed to the door, her hands frantically searching for a mechanism, a latch, anything that could open it. The smooth stone offered no answers, no visible means of entry. Her frustration mounted as the sounds of pursuit grew louder, the men's voices now echoing in the chamber behind her.

"Come on," she whispered, slamming her palm against the door. "There has to be a way."

Her eyes darted back to the carvings on the walls. The symbols seemed to pulse faintly, as if responding to her presence. The connection was undeniable—the crystal, the talisman, the carvings—they were all part of the same ancient system. Lena reached for the pendant around her neck, her fingers trembling as she lifted it toward the door.

The moment the pendant touched the stone, a surge of energy coursed through her. The carvings flared to life, their glow intensifying as the air around her seemed to vibrate. A deep rumble echoed through the chamber, and Lena felt the door shift beneath her hand.

Slowly, with a groan that reverberated through the temple, the stone door began to slide open.

Lena didn't wait. She slipped through the narrow opening just as the men entered the chamber, their footsteps faltering at the sight of the glowing carvings.

"She's using it," one of them growled. "Stop her!"

The door slammed shut behind Lena, cutting off their shouts. She allowed herself a single breath of relief before continuing down the narrow passage beyond. The air was damp, the walls closing in around her as she pressed forward. She didn't know where the passage led, but anything was better than being cornered in the chamber.

The tunnel eventually opened into a small alcove, its walls lined with what appeared to be ancient tools and artifacts. Lena paused, her eyes scanning the space for anything useful. Her fingers brushed against a weathered tablet, its surface etched with more of the strange symbols she had seen throughout the temple. She didn't have time to decipher them now, but something told her they were important.

The sound of approaching footsteps jolted her back into motion. The men had found another way through.

Lena grabbed the tablet and bolted toward the alcove's far exit, her legs protesting as she pushed herself harder. The jungle air hit her like a wall as she emerged from the temple, the dense foliage swallowing her up. She didn't stop, weaving through the undergrowth with the tablet clutched tightly to her chest.

The jungle was alive with movement, every rustle of leaves or snap of a branch sending her heart into overdrive. She couldn't tell if the sounds were natural or if her pursuers were closing in, but she didn't dare slow down to find out.

Her feet slipped on the damp ground, and she nearly lost her balance as she descended a steep incline. The tablet slipped from her grasp, landing with a soft thud in the mud. Lena scrambled to retrieve it, her fingers shaking as she wiped the muck away.

And then she heard it—a low growl, deep and guttural, cutting through the jungle's symphony of noise.

Lena froze, her eyes scanning the shadows. The growl came again, closer this time. Her breath caught in her throat as a pair of glowing eyes appeared in the darkness, their predatory gaze locked onto her.

A jaguar.

The sleek, muscular form of the animal emerged from the shadows, its movements slow and deliberate. Lena's pulse thundered in her ears as she backed away, her mind racing. She couldn't outrun it, and she certainly couldn't fight it.

The jaguar snarled, its body tensed as if ready to pounce. Lena's hand instinctively went to the pendant around her neck, her fingers gripping it tightly. The hum of the talisman resonated through her, and she felt a surge of energy—a faint echo of the crystal's power.

"Please," she whispered, her voice trembling. "Help me."

The pendant pulsed, its light flaring briefly. The jaguar hesitated, its growl fading into a low rumble. For a moment, it seemed to regard her with curiosity, its head tilting slightly.

Then, without warning, it turned and melted back into the shadows, leaving Lena trembling but unharmed.

She didn't have time to process what had just happened. The shouts of her pursuers cut through the jungle, spurring her back into motion. Lena clutched the tablet and ran, her determination renewed.

She didn't know how far she would have to go, but she knew one thing for certain: she couldn't stop. Not until she was safe. Not until she had unraveled the crystal's mysteries.

The chase was far from over, but Lena was ready for whatever came next.

Lena sprinted through the dense underbrush, the jungle closing in around her with every step. The thick canopy above allowed only fragmented beams of light to pierce through, creating an eerie glow. Her lungs burned with every breath, and her legs screamed in protest, but she didn't dare stop. The voices of her pursuers echoed behind her, relentless and closing the gap.

The tablet she had grabbed earlier felt heavier with every step, its edges digging into her hands as she clutched it tightly. She hadn't had time to examine it, but something deep inside her told her it was important—a piece of the puzzle she was desperately trying to solve. The ancient carvings on its surface pulsed faintly, as if alive, in sync with the talisman around her neck.

The shouts grew louder, and Lena risked a glance over her shoulder. The two men were now visible through the foliage, their dark clothing blending almost seamlessly with the shadows of the jungle. One of them barked an order, and the other raised what looked like a gun.

Lena ducked instinctively as a dart as a dart from a tranquilizer gun whizzed past her ear, embedding itself into the bark of a nearby tree. Her heart skipped a beat, fear coursing through her veins like wildfire. They weren't trying to kill her—at least, not yet. They wanted her alive. For the crystal? The talisman? She couldn't be sure, but she knew she couldn't let them catch her.

She pushed herself harder, zigzagging through the trees in an attempt to make herself a harder target. Her foot caught on a protruding root, and she stumbled, barely managing to stay upright. The tablet slipped from her grasp, tumbling to the ground.

"No!" she gasped, dropping to her knees to retrieve it.

Her fingers closed around the artifact just as another dart shot past her, narrowly missing her shoulder. She scrambled back to her feet, clutching the tablet to her chest, and took off again. The terrain grew steeper, the ground uneven and slippery from the morning's rain. She could hear the rushing sound of water ahead—maybe a river? If she could make it there, she might have a chance to lose them.

The jungle opened up suddenly, revealing a fast-moving river cutting through the dense foliage. The water churned violently, its surface broken by jagged rocks. Lena skidded to a halt at the edge, her chest heaving as she surveyed her options. The river was dangerous, but the men were close—too close.

She didn't have a choice.

Clutching the tablet and talisman tightly, she leaped into the water.

The icy shock of the river stole her breath, and the current immediately pulled her under. She fought to surface, gasping for air as the torrent carried her downstream. The tablet threatened to slip from her grasp, but she held on, refusing to let it go. The talisman around her neck glowed faintly, its warmth a stark contrast to the freezing water.

Above the roar of the river, she could hear the shouts of the men as they reached the riverbank. One of them aimed his weapon at her, but the current carried her out of range before he could fire.

Lena's head dipped below the surface again as the river dragged her toward a sharp bend. She flailed, her arms aching from the effort of keeping herself and the tablet above water. The rocks loomed ahead, and she knew she had to act fast if she wanted to avoid being smashed against them.

With every ounce of strength she had left, Lena reached for an overhanging branch as she was swept past it. Her fingers closed around the slick wood, and she held on for dear life, the current tugging at her body as if determined to pull her back in. Gritting her teeth, she hauled herself toward the riverbank, her muscles screaming in protest.

Finally, she collapsed onto the muddy shore, coughing and gasping for air. Her entire body trembled from the cold and exertion, but she was alive. The tablet was still in her hands, and the talisman around her neck pulsed faintly, as if reassuring her that she had made the right choice.

Lena lay there for a moment, catching her breath, before forcing herself to sit up. She couldn't stay here. The men wouldn't give up so easily—they would find a way to follow her. She needed to move.

The jungle around her was eerily quiet, save for the distant rush of the river. The trees loomed tall and imposing, their branches intertwining to form a near-impenetrable canopy. Lena pushed herself to her feet, her body protesting every movement, and began to walk.

Her mind raced as she navigated the dense undergrowth. Who were those men? How had they known about the crystal and the talisman? And why were they so determined to capture her? The shaman's warnings echoed in her mind: *There are others who seek the crystal. Others who would use its power for their own purposes.*

But why her? Why was everything happening now? Why had she been chosen?

The tablet felt warm against her hands, its carvings glowing faintly in the dim light. She stopped to examine it more closely, her fingers tracing the intricate symbols etched into its surface. They were similar to the ones she had seen in the temple, and yet, there was something different about them—something that felt more... specific.

Lena frowned, trying to decipher their meaning. The symbols seemed to depict a map, but not of any landscape she recognized. It was abstract, almost geometric, with lines and shapes that intersected in strange, complex patterns. At the center of the design was a circular symbol that looked strikingly similar to the crystal.

The realization hit her like a thunderclap.

This wasn't just a map. It was a guide—a blueprint for unlocking the crystal's true potential. The shaman had said the crystal was a key, but Lena had never understood what it was meant to unlock. Now, she was beginning to see the bigger picture.

Before she could process it further, a rustling in the bushes snapped her back to reality. Lena's grip on the tablet tightened as she turned toward the sound, her heart pounding.

A figure emerged from the shadows, and Lena's stomach dropped.

It was Ruiz.

His face was pale, his expression torn between anger and desperation. He raised his hands, palms out, as if trying to reassure her.

"Lena," he said, his voice strained. "I'm not here to hurt you. But you need to listen to me."

Lena took a step back, her eyes narrowing. "Why are you here? Were you with them?"

Ruiz hesitated, his gaze darting toward the direction of the river. "It's complicated. I didn't know who they were at first, but I realized too late. They're part of an organization—people who've been searching for the crystal for decades. They believe it's the key to controlling time itself."

"And you just happened to be working with them?" Lena shot back, her voice sharp. "You lied to me."

"I didn't know," Ruiz insisted, his voice pleading. "They approached me years ago, asking for my help with their research. I thought it was legitimate—until I saw what they were willing to do to get what they wanted."

Lena's grip on the tablet didn't loosen. "Why should I believe you?"

"Because I'm here, aren't I?" Ruiz said, his tone urgent. "I left them. I came to warn you. They'll stop at nothing to control the crystal—and the power it holds."

Lena's heart raced as she weighed his words. She didn't trust him, but she couldn't deny the fear in his eyes. For now, she had no choice but to keep moving—and to stay one step ahead of those who sought to control the crystal.

Chapter 14: Ancient Knowledge

The firelight flickered, casting shadows that danced across the ancient texts spread out before Lena. The symbols etched into the worn pages seemed to come alive under the warm glow, whispering secrets only she could hear. Around her, the jungle remained quiet, a watchful guardian over the mysteries hidden within. Lena had always felt a pull toward the unknown, but now, with the crystal's hum resonating in her chest and the Talisman pulsing faintly against her skin, the pull felt almost magnetic.

Ruiz sat on the other side of the fire, his gaze distant as he processed the enormity of their situation. He seemed lost in thought, perhaps reflecting on the events that had brought them here—the chase, the betrayal, and the escape. His earlier revelations about the ancient civilization's mastery over time had shaken Lena, but they had also given her clarity.

The people who created the crystal clock hadn't been like anyone Lena had studied before. They were more advanced than any civilization she had ever read about, their knowledge surpassing the boundaries of science and veering into something almost divine. But their downfall was clear: they had meddled too much, pushed too far, and ultimately paid the price. The warnings etched in their texts now felt like a personal message, a plea for restraint.

The Ancient Texts

Lena reached for one of the manuscripts, her fingers trembling slightly as she traced the delicate symbols carved into the brittle parchment. They were intricate and hypnotic, a blend of geometric precision and organic fluidity that defied categorization. The shapes seemed to vibrate beneath her touch, as if the knowledge within them was alive.

"This," Lena began, breaking the silence, "isn't just history. It's a guide." Her voice was steady, but a tremor of awe lingered in her words.

Ruiz leaned forward, his interest piqued. "A guide? To what?"

"To the crystal," Lena replied. "Look at this." She held the manuscript up to the firelight, revealing a diagram that appeared to map the flow of time. Lines intersected in intricate patterns, creating a web of possibilities, all radiating outward from a central point—the crystal itself.

Ruiz frowned, studying the text. "This looks like… like a representation of causality. Cause and effect."

"Exactly." Lena nodded, her mind racing. "It's a map of how time flows, how every action ripples outward to create consequences. The crystal isn't just a key—it's the center of everything. The ancients must have used it to manipulate time, to shift these pathways."

Ruiz's eyes widened. "If that's true, then the crystal isn't just a tool. It's the very heart of time itself."

Lena swallowed hard, the weight of his words settling over her like a heavy cloak. The crystal wasn't just powerful—it was fundamental. A force of nature, bound to the very fabric of reality. And now, it was her responsibility.

The Warning of Balance

The fire crackled softly as Lena turned to another section of the text. This one was different, darker. The symbols were more jagged, the flow of the writing more frantic, as though the scribe had been desperate to convey a warning. Her eyes scanned the page, the meaning slowly unraveling before her.

"They feared it," she murmured, her voice barely audible.

Ruiz looked up sharply. "What do you mean?"

Lena pointed to the text. "They realized too late what they had created. The crystal gave them the ability to control time, but with that power came consequences. Every time they used it to change the past or shape the future, they caused unintended ripple effects—disasters, collapses, entire civilizations erased from existence. They couldn't control it. I think that every time they used it to alter and then fix time, they could only go back in time to fix what they had damaged. Every change had unintended consequences and they eventually destroyed themselves."

Lena pondered on what she had just said and then she realized, "we can alter time and look ahead into the future to see what we have done. The problem is if we get it wrong, we need to keep going back into the past to fix everything. If we get it wrong, we destroy everything eventually."

Ruiz's face darkened. "So they abandoned it."

"They didn't just abandon it," Lena continued, her voice growing more urgent. "They sealed it away. They created guardians, beings who were connected to the crystal, who could protect it from those who might misuse it."

Ruiz's gaze shifted to the Talisman hanging around her neck. "And you're one of them."

The statement hung in the air, heavy with implication. Lena didn't deny it but responded, "I think so." She had felt the connection from the moment she first touched the crystal. It wasn't just an artifact to her—it was a part of her, a piece of something much larger.

The Shaman's Insight

Lena's thoughts drifted back to the shaman's words. *You are the key, Lena. The crystal has chosen you, but the path ahead will not be easy.* At the time, she hadn't fully understood what he meant. But now, as she sat surrounded by the knowledge of an ancient civilization, the weight of his words became clearer.

"The shaman knew," Lena said aloud, breaking the silence. "He understood what this meant, what the crystal was capable of. That's why he gave me the matched Talisman to what I had from Mrs. Harrison. It's not just a tool—it's a connection. A way to channel the crystal's power without losing control."

Ruiz nodded slowly, his expression thoughtful. "That makes sense. If the crystal is as powerful as these texts suggest, then the Talisman would act as a kind of... buffer. A safeguard to keep the power from overwhelming you."

"But it's more than that," Lena added. "The Talisman and the crystal are two halves of the same whole. Without the Talisman, the crystal's power is unstable. And without the crystal, the Talisman is incomplete. They were always meant to be together."

Ruiz's expression grew somber. "Which means the people chasing us won't stop until they have both."

The Eternal Conflict

The realization hit Lena like a thunderbolt. The men who had pursued her weren't just after the crystal—they were after control. Control over time, over reality itself. And if they succeeded, the consequences would be catastrophic.

"We can't let them have it," Lena said firmly, her resolve hardening. "No matter what."

Ruiz nodded, his jaw tightening. "Agreed. But how do we stop them? They're organized, well-funded. And we're just... us."

Lena glanced down at the Talisman, its faint glow a reminder of the power she now wielded. "We don't need an army. We have control of the crystal, and we have the knowledge of the people who created it. That's more than enough."

"But it's also dangerous," Ruiz countered. "The more we use the crystal, the greater the risk of creating ripples we can't control. We need to be careful."

Lena met his gaze, her eyes steady. "I understand the risks. But if we don't act, they'll take it from us. And if that happens, the world as we know it could be destroyed."

Ruiz sighed, rubbing his temples. "Then we need a plan. A way to stay ahead of them while we figure out how to keep the crystal safe."

A Glimmer of Hope

As the night deepened, Lena and Ruiz pored over the texts, searching for anything that could give them an advantage. The ancient civilization had left behind more than warnings—they had left behind hope. Hidden within the texts were clues, fragments of knowledge that pointed to a way to control the crystal's power without risking the collapse of reality.

"It's like a lock and key," Lena said, her voice tinged with excitement. "The crystal's energy flows in a specific pattern, like a circuit. If we can understand that pattern, we can use the crystal without destabilizing time."

Ruiz frowned, his brow furrowed. "But how do we figure out the pattern? These texts are incomplete, and we don't have the tools to decode them fully."

Lena's hand brushed against the Talisman, and an idea sparked in her mind. "Maybe we don't need the tools. Maybe the Talisman is the key."

She held the Talisman up to the firelight, its intricate carvings casting shadows on the pages below. The symbols on the Talisman seemed to align perfectly with those in the text, as though they were two pieces of a puzzle.

Ruiz leaned closer, his eyes widening. "You're right. The Talisman... it's a guide. It's showing us how to unlock the crystal's true potential."

Lena's heart raced as the pieces began to fall into place. The crystal, the Talisman, the texts—they were all connected, part of a larger plan. The ancient civilization had left behind the tools needed to protect the crystal, to ensure its power would never fall into the wrong hands.

And now, that responsibility rested with her.

As the fire burned low, casting long shadows across the campsite, Lena felt a renewed sense of purpose. The road ahead would be dangerous, but she wasn't afraid. She had the knowledge of the ancients, the power of the crystal, and the determination to see this through.

She would protect the crystal. She needed protect time itself.

The silence of the jungle enveloped the camp, broken only by the occasional stir of nocturnal animals. The ancient texts and diagrams scattered across the makeshift table before Lena felt alive, their symbols glowing faintly under the firelight. The Talisman in her hands vibrated gently, as though responding to the energy coursing through her thoughts. She couldn't shake the feeling that her path was now clearer—but infinitely more perilous.

Ruiz, sitting opposite her, leaned back, his face pale from exhaustion. The professor, usually calm and composed, now wore an expression of unease that mirrored Lena's own. They both knew the gravity of the situation."We need to move soon," Ruiz said, breaking the silence. "If those men find us again, we won't have the element of surprise. And from what I saw in their eyes, they won't stop until they have the crystal. Or worse, the Talisman."

Lena nodded, her fingers absentmindedly tracing the intricate carvings on the pendant. "They know what it's capable of, but they don't understand it—not fully. They only see the power it could give them. The way it could tip the scales in their favor. But this isn't a weapon they can wield without consequence."

Ruiz's expression darkened. "No, it's not. And that's what makes them so dangerous. People who don't understand the risks are the most likely to misuse it."

■■

Unlocking the Knowledge of the Ancients

Lena's eyes shifted back to the text in front of her. The diagrams of time's flow, the depictions of the crystal clock, and the instructions on the Talisman's alignment—they all pointed to a single purpose: preserving the balance. The ancients had seen the destruction unchecked power could unleash, and they had taken steps to protect the world from it.

But the texts weren't complete. Pages were missing, torn away by time or by those who had sought to bury the knowledge. Still, the fragments that remained were enough to hint at the crystal's full potential.

"The Talisman and the crystal," Lena said aloud, her voice quiet but firm, "they're more than just tools. They're safeguards. The ancients created them as a way to regulate time's flow, to prevent the kind of chaos that could unravel everything."

Ruiz leaned forward, his curiosity piqued. "And the guardians? How do they fit into this?"

Lena hesitated, her fingers brushing over a passage she had translated earlier. The text described individuals chosen by the crystal—individuals who could hear its call, who were uniquely attuned to its energy. They were meant to protect it, to ensure that its power was never misused.

"I think..." Lena began, her voice trailing off. "I think the guardians are like conduits. They don't control the crystal's power; they amplify it. But that also means they share its burden. If the crystal's energy becomes unstable, the guardian suffers too."

Ruiz's eyes widened in realization. "That's why the Talisman is so important. It acts as a stabilizer, keeping the guardian and the crystal in sync."

Lena nodded. "Without it, the crystal's power could overwhelm the guardian—or worse, it could fracture completely. That's probably what happened to the ancients. They pushed the crystal too far, and the balance broke."

The Enemy's Intentions

The thought sent a shiver down Lena's spine. She had felt the crystal's power firsthand—the way it pulsed through her, the way it seemed to resonate with her very soul. But she had also felt its instability, the cracks in its energy that threatened to spiral out of control. If the crystal fell into the wrong hands, the results would be catastrophic.

And then there was the matter of the enemy. The men who had chased her through the jungle, who had nearly captured her, weren't ordinary treasure hunters. They were organized, methodical, and ruthless. Lena had seen the greed in their eyes, but there had been something else too—fear. Fear of what would happen if they failed to retrieve the crystal and the Talisman.

"They're working for someone," Lena said suddenly, the realization hitting her like a bolt of lightning. "Those men—this isn't just about them. They're taking orders."

Ruiz frowned. "I agree, but orders from who? And why?"

"I don't know," Lena admitted. "But whoever it is, they know about the crystal. They know about the Talisman. And they're willing to do whatever it takes to get them."

Ruiz's jaw tightened. "Then we have to stay ahead of them. If they catch up to us—"

"They won't," Lena interrupted, her voice firm. "I won't let them."

Preparing for What's Next

Lena's resolve hardened as she gathered the ancient texts and secured them in her pack. The Talisman, still warm against her chest, felt like a lifeline. It was a reminder of the responsibility she bore, but also of the power she carried within her.

"We need to find the missing pieces," she said, turning to Ruiz. "The texts are incomplete, but there has to be more out there. The ancients wouldn't have left this knowledge scattered without a way to find it."

Ruiz hesitated, then nodded. "If there are more texts, they're likely hidden in places like the temple. Remote, isolated sites where they could be protected from anyone who sought to exploit them."

"Then that's where we'll go," Lena said, her determination unwavering. "The more we understand, the better chance we have of keeping the crystal safe."

As the fire burned low and the first hints of dawn painted the horizon, Lena and Ruiz began to pack their belongings. The jungle around them stirred with the sounds of awakening life, a stark contrast to the quiet tension that hung between them.

Lena tightened her grip on the Talisman, its pulse steady and reassuring. She didn't know what lay ahead, but she knew one thing for certain: the crystal had chosen her for a reason. And she wouldn't let it down.

As they prepared to move out, Lena cast one last glance at the sky, the faint glow of the crystal still lingering in her mind. The path ahead was uncertain, but she was ready to face it.

The ancient knowledge would guide her.

And she would protect the balance, no matter the cost.

Chapter 15: The Enemy Unmasked

Lena was beginning to feel like she was sorting out the mysteries. Then from nowhere, a figure appeared. Both Lena and Ruiz were startled.

"I'm Masita" said the voice. "You can call me the Keeper. I am here to warn you."

The tension in the air was suffocating as the Keeper paced, her sharp gaze darting toward every shadow that flickered across the ancient walls of the ruined city. Lena stood by her side, her fingers brushing the smooth surface of the pendant around her neck. She could feel its pulse—a rhythmic thrum that matched her heartbeat—as if the Talisman were alive, warning her of the storm to come.

"They'll come tonight," the Keeper said, her voice low and deliberate. "The Weavers are drawn to shifts in the timeline. Every ripple you've caused has led them here."

Ruiz asked the Keeper, "what can I do to help?" She responded by asking, "please go tell the others their work is done here. "Stay at the village for now."

Lena's throat tightened. She had felt the timeline bending ever since her use of the crystal, but the knowledge that she had inadvertently lured the Weavers filled her with dread. The Keeper had warned her about them—ancient beings who existed between the strands of time itself. They were neither entirely human nor entirely other, their power tied to the manipulation of time in ways Lena was only beginning to understand.

"Who are they really?" Lena asked, her voice barely above a whisper. "What do they want?"

The Keeper paused, turning to face her. "The Weavers are remnants of a forgotten age, bound to the timeline but never part of it. They once guarded time's flow, but their purpose twisted. Now, they seek to control it, to weave it into patterns of their choosing. They are not bound by morality or balance, only by their insatiable hunger for power."

Lena swallowed hard, her mind racing. She had always known she was part of something larger than herself, but the scale of it was staggering. She wasn't just protecting the crystal or a single moment in time—she was standing against an ancient force that had the power to unravel everything in the universe.

As the night deepened, the ruined city grew eerily quiet. The distant hum of life that usually surrounded them had faded, replaced by an oppressive stillness. Even the air seemed to vibrate, charged with an invisible energy.

And then, they came.

The Arrival of the Weavers

At first, Lena saw nothing. The shadows danced in the moonlight, shifting like whispers at the edges of her vision. But then she felt it—a disturbance in the air, as if the fabric of reality was being stretched thin. The temperature dropped, and a faint, otherworldly light began to seep through the cracks in the ruins.

They emerged from the shadows, their forms shimmering like heatwaves. The Weavers were taller than Lena had imagined, their movements fluid yet unnatural. Their bodies seemed to flicker in and out of existence, as if they were not entirely tethered to the present. Their eyes glowed a faint blue, piercing and cold, and their hands crackled with energy that distorted the space around them.

"You've meddled with forces you do not understand," one of them hissed, his voice a distorted echo. "The timeline bends to us. You cannot undo what you've done."

Lena's hand tightened around the pendant. "You don't own time," she said, her voice steady despite the fear that coiled in her chest. "It belongs to no one."

The Weaver tilted his head, his glowing eyes narrowing. "And yet you wield its power as if it were yours to control. You've already upset the balance. We are here to take it back."

The Keeper stepped forward, her presence a beacon of defiance. "Time belongs to itself. You will not twist it to your will."

The Weavers laughed, their voices merging into a dissonant chorus that sent shivers down Lena's spine. "Fools. You think you can stand against us? We are the Weavers, and we exist beyond the threads you cling to."

The Battle Begins

Without warning, the Weavers moved, their forms blurring as they closed the distance. The air around them warped, shimmering with raw energy that made Lena's skin prickle. The Keeper reacted instantly, her hands weaving intricate patterns in the air. Time itself seemed to shift around her, creating barriers that slowed the Weavers' approach.

"Focus!" the Keeper shouted. "Use the Talisman—feel its connection to the timeline!"

Lena nodded, her pulse racing. She reached for the pendant, letting its energy flow through her. The hum grew louder, resonating with the vibrations in the air. She could feel the threads of time stretching around her, intertwining and pulsing with life.

The first Weaver lunged toward her, his hand outstretched, crackling with energy. Instinctively, Lena raised her hand, and a wave of force erupted from the Talisman. The Weaver staggered, his form flickering as he struggled to regain control.

But there were more.

Two more Weavers appeared, their movements swift and unpredictable. They manipulated the timeline around them, distorting reality and creating fractures in the air. Lena felt the ground shift beneath her feet, moments slipping out of sync as the Weavers' power took hold.

"You cannot win," one of them said, his voice a chilling whisper. "You are but a fleeting moment, lost in the vastness of eternity."

Lena gritted her teeth. "Maybe. But even a moment can change everything."

Unlocking the Power

As the battle raged, Lena's connection to the Talisman deepened. She could feel its energy merging with hers, guiding her movements and amplifying her instincts. The threads of time became visible to her—a shimmering web of light that stretched in all directions. She reached out, grasping one of the threads, and felt its power surge through her.

The Weavers hesitated, their glowing eyes narrowing as they sensed the shift in her. "You're stronger than we thought," one of them murmured. "But strength alone will not save you."

Lena ignored him. She focused on the threads, weaving them together with her mind, pulling them tight to create a barrier between herself and the Weavers. The air around her shimmered, and the fractures they had created began to mend.

The Keeper fought beside her, her movements precise and deliberate. Together, they pushed back the Weavers, their combined power disrupting the enemy's control over the timeline. But the Weavers were relentless, their attacks growing more desperate as they realized the tide was turning.

Lena reached deeper into the Talisman's power, drawing on the crystal's connection to the very essence of time. She could feel the timeline stabilizing, the fractures healing as her energy flowed through them. The Weavers screamed in frustration, their forms flickering as their grip on reality weakened.

The Final Blow

"You've meddled long enough," Lena said, her voice steady and commanding. "Time isn't yours to control."

With a final surge of energy, she reached out and wove the threads of time around the Weavers, trapping them in a loop they could not escape. The air crackled with power as the timeline stabilized, sealing the Weavers in a prison of their own making.

The ruins fell silent. The Weavers were gone, their presence erased from the timeline. Lena collapsed to her knees, her chest heaving as she tried to catch her breath.

The Keeper knelt beside her, a faint smile on her lips. "You did it," she said softly. "You've proven yourself, Lena. You're stronger than I ever imagined."

Lena looked up at her, exhaustion etched into her features. "But at what cost? The timeline... the crystal... it's all so fragile."

The Keeper placed a hand on her shoulder. "You've restored balance. That's all that matters for now."

Lena nodded, though the weight of her actions still pressed heavily on her. She had faced the Weavers and won, but she knew this was not the end. Time was vast and unpredictable, and the forces that sought to control it were relentless.

As the first light of dawn broke over the ruins, Lena stood, her resolve strengthening. She was the guardian of time, and her journey was far from over. The Weavers had been defeated, but the echoes of their presence lingered, a reminder that the battle for time's balance was never truly won.

Lena tightened her grip on the Talisman and turned toward the horizon. She didn't know what lay ahead, but she was ready to face it. For now, time was safe—and she intended to keep it that way.

The Calm After the Storm

The ruins were quiet, save for the distant sounds of the jungle beginning to stir with the morning light. Lena stood in the middle of the ancient stone chamber, her fingers still wrapped around the Talisman that pulsed faintly against her chest. The battle was over, the Weavers defeated, but her body still buzzed with the adrenaline of the fight. She could feel the threads of time settling back into place, their once chaotic rhythm smoothing into a steady flow. For now, balance had been restored.

The Keeper moved to her side, her gaze fixed on the faint glow of the Talisman. "The timeline is healing," she said, her voice quiet but firm. "You've done what many thought was impossible. You've stopped the Weavers."

Lena nodded, though her thoughts were far from celebratory. "Are they gone?" she asked, her voice laced with uncertainty. "Or have we just delayed them?"

The Keeper hesitated before responding. "The prison you wove is strong, but the Weavers are not like us. They exist outside the bounds of time in ways we don't fully understand. You've trapped them in a loop, a fracture they cannot escape for now. But forever… I cannot say."

Lena's shoulders sagged. She wanted to believe they were gone for good, that she had truly defeated them, but doubt lingered. The Weavers were powerful, and their hunger for control had been palpable. If they had been drawn to the crystal's power once, what was to stop them from finding another way back?

"I hope they're gone," Lena murmured, her gaze distant. "I hope they're trapped in their loop, lost in time forever."

The Keeper placed a hand on her shoulder, grounding her. "What you've done is enough for now. The timeline is stable, and the Weavers are no longer a threat. You've given time the space to heal."

Reflections in the Aftermath

As the sun climbed higher, casting golden light over the ruins, Lena and the Keeper began to leave the ancient city. The air felt lighter now, the oppressive weight of the Weavers' presence gone. But as they walked, Lena's mind churned with questions.

"The Weavers said time bends to them," Lena said, breaking the silence. "That they could control it. Do you think… do you think they were guardians once, like you said? Did they start with good intentions?"

The Keeper sighed, her expression contemplative. "It's possible. Time is a force unlike any other—unforgiving, yet malleable in the wrong hands. Those who seek to master it are often consumed by their ambition. The Weavers may have been like you once, chosen by the crystal to protect the timeline. But somewhere along the way, they lost their way."

Lena considered this, her grip tightening on the Talisman. "What if the same thing happens to me? What if I make the wrong choice and become like them?"

The Keeper stopped, turning to face her. "You won't," she said firmly. "Because you've already made the hardest choice—to protect, not to control. The Weavers sought power. You seek balance. That is what sets you apart."

Lena nodded, though the fear still lingered at the edges of her mind. She didn't want to become like the Weavers, but the power she had wielded—the sheer force of time bending to her will—was intoxicating. She would have to remain vigilant, to resist the temptation to use the crystal for anything other than protecting the timeline.

A Flicker of Uncertainty

By the time they reached the outskirts of the jungle, Lena felt the pull of the crystal again, faint but insistent. It was as though it were calling to her, a whisper she couldn't quite decipher. She paused, her gaze drifting back toward the direction of the ruins.

"What is it?" the Keeper asked, her tone sharp.

Lena hesitated. "I don't know. It feels… like something is still there. Like the crystal is trying to tell me something."

The Keeper frowned. "The crystal's power is dormant for now. What you're feeling may be an echo of your connection to it."

But Lena wasn't so sure. The feeling wasn't just an echo—it was alive, pulsing faintly at the edges of her consciousness. It was as if the crystal was warning her of something she couldn't yet see.

"I hope you're right," Lena said quietly, turning away from the ruins. "I hope the Weavers are gone for good. But if they aren't…"

She trailed off, her thoughts too tangled to put into words. The Keeper didn't press her, but Lena could feel the weight of her gaze.

A New Resolve

As the two of them made their way back toward the village, Lena felt a shift within herself. The doubts, the fear—they were still there, but beneath them was something stronger. Resolve. Determination. She had faced the Weavers and survived. She had protected the timeline, and she would do it again if she had to.

The Talisman throbbed faintly against her chest, a reminder of the power she had been entrusted with. It was both a gift and a burden, and Lena knew she would have to carry it for the rest of her life. But she wasn't alone. The Keeper had taught her that much.

As they reached the edge of the village, the Keeper turned to her. "Your journey is far from over, Lena," she said. "The crystal's power is bound to you, and with that comes responsibility. But you've proven yourself. You are ready for what's to come."

Lena nodded, her gaze steady. "If the Weavers return, I'll be ready for them. And if there are others like them… I'll stop them too."

The Keeper smiled faintly. "Good. But remember, Lena, the crystal's power is not just about stopping others. It's about maintaining balance. Protect the timeline, yes, but don't forget to live within it too."

The words struck a chord in Lena, and she felt a flicker of hope. Maybe, just maybe, she could find a way to carry this burden without losing herself.

As the sun dipped lower, casting long shadows over the mountains, Lena allowed herself a small smile. The Weavers were gone, at least for now, and the timeline was safe. But if they ever returned, she would be ready.

For now, she walked forward, her Talisman humming faintly against her chest—a reminder of the power within her and the responsibility she carried.

The hum of time itself was back, steady and constant, and Lena felt a renewed sense of purpose. The future was uncertain, but she wasn't afraid. Whatever lay ahead, she would face it head-on.

The guardian of time, ready for whatever came next.

Chapter 16: The Power Within

Lena returned to the Crystal the next day.

The air in the temple was heavy, the weight of centuries of silence pressing down like a shroud. The only sound was the faint hum of the crystal, resonating through the chamber like a heartbeat, steady and eternal. Lena stood in the center, her chest rising and falling as she prepared herself. The moment had come. She wasn't just defending the crystal; she was embracing a power she could barely comprehend, a force that had chosen her and her alone.

Her fingers brushed the Talisman around her neck, the warmth of its energy coursing through her like a steady current. She could feel the crystal's pull, its pulse synchronizing with her own. The connection was deeper now, stronger. The line between her and the crystal was no longer distinct—they were one.

Lena closed her eyes, letting the energy flow through her, and with it came clarity. She had seen the visions, glimpses of the past and future. She understood now that time wasn't linear but fluid, a living, breathing entity that needed to be protected. It wasn't about control; it was about balance.

She opened her eyes. The crystal pulsed in the dim light, illuminating the ancient carvings on the walls. They told a story of guardians before her, those who had protected the crystal from those who sought to abuse its power. But now, it was her turn. She had to prove herself worthy.

The Confrontation

Footsteps echoed from the entrance, steady and deliberate. Lena's heart quickened, but she didn't move. She knew who it was. It was Dr. Montgomery from her University and his team who had been relentless, their hunger for the crystal's power driving them to pursue her across the jungle and into the depths of the temple. They were hired to feed the corporate greed in the world.

"Lena," Montgomery's voice called, sharp and commanding. His silhouette appeared in the archway, flanked by two of his men. They entered the chamber, their eyes immediately locking onto the crystal. "Step away."

Lena turned to face them, her hand still resting on the crystal's surface. Its energy surged beneath her touch, filling her with strength. "So you are the one giving orders to these thugs. You don't understand what you're dealing with," she said, her voice calm but firm. "This isn't just an artifact. It's alive. It's connected to everything—time, space, existence. You can't just take it."

Montgomery's lips curled into a smirk. "You think you're the only one who understands it? You're a child playing with forces you can't control. This power doesn't belong to you. It belongs to humanity. To progress."

"Progress?" Lena shot back. "Or destruction? You don't care about balance or consequences. You just want power."

One of Montgomery's men stepped forward, his hand resting on the weapon holstered at his hip. "We don't have time for this," he growled. "Take her down, and we'll deal with the crystal ourselves."

But Montgomery raised a hand, stopping him. "No. She's connected to it. We need her alive—for now."

The Power Awakens

Lena felt the crystal's hum grow stronger, as though it were responding to their threat. She could feel its energy flowing into her, amplifying her senses, sharpening her focus. The Talisman around her neck glowed faintly, and she realized that the crystal was offering her a choice. Fight or flee.

She chose to fight.

With a deep breath, Lena raised her hand, her fingers outstretched. The energy within her surged, and the air around her seemed to shift. Time itself responded to her will, slowing to a crawl. Montgomery and his men froze mid-step, their movements caught in the invisible web she had cast.

The room was silent, the world suspended. Lena moved through the stillness, her footsteps echoing faintly in the frozen moment. She approached Montgomery, her gaze steady. "You don't understand what you're trying to take," she said softly, though she knew he couldn't hear her. "You think this is a weapon. But it's so much more than that."

She released her hold, and time snapped back into motion. Montgomery stumbled, his eyes widening as he realized what had just happened. "What did you—?"

"You can't take this from me," Lena interrupted. "The crystal has chosen me, and I won't let you destroy what it's meant to protect."

The Battle of Wills

Montgomery's men didn't hesitate this time. They charged toward her, weapons drawn, their intentions clear. A shot was fired at Lena and before she could react everything around her stopped. Everything was frozen and the bullet fired at Lena stopped just inches from her chest. A shot that would have been fatal if it hit her. The crystal's power coursed through her, heightening her reflexes and sharpening her mind. The crystal had saved her life. She raised her hand again, and time bent to her will.

The attackers froze mid-motion, their weapons suspended in the air. Lena moved around them, her movements deliberate. She could see every detail—the sweat on their brows, the tension in their muscles. She knew that this power was dangerous, but she also knew it was the only way to protect the crystal.

With a wave of her hand, she pushed them back, sending them stumbling to the ground as time resumed its normal flow. They looked at her with a mixture of fear and awe, their confidence shaken.

Montgomery, however, was undeterred. "You can't stop us forever," he said, his voice low and dangerous. "You think you've won, but you're just delaying the inevitable."

Lena shook her head. "This isn't about winning. It's about protecting something that's bigger than all of us."

The Crystal's Judgment

As Montgomery lunged toward the crystal, Lena felt the Talisman around her neck pulse with energy. She stepped forward, placing herself between him and the artifact. The crystal flared brightly, its light filling the chamber and forcing Montgomery to shield his eyes.

"You don't understand what you're doing!" he shouted, his voice strained. "You can't control it!"

"I'm not trying to control it," Lena replied. "I'm listening to it."

The crystal's energy surged, enveloping Lena in a cocoon of light. She felt its power flowing through her, guiding her, showing her what needed to be done. She raised her hands, and the room seemed to tremble as the crystal's hum grew louder.

Montgomery and his men were thrown back, their weapons clattering to the ground. The crystal's light grew brighter, its energy pushing them to the edge of the chamber. Lena could feel its judgment, its decision. It was protecting itself—and her.

When the light finally dimmed, the men were gone, banished from the temple. The chamber was quiet once more, the only sound the soft hum of the crystal. Lena felt that the men had be sent away to a prison locked between the moments of time. A moment that they would never escape from.

The Guardian's Promise

Lena sank to her knees, the weight of what had just happened settling over her. The crystal's energy was still with her, but she knew it was a power she couldn't take lightly. She had been given a gift, but also a responsibility.

She reached out, her hand resting on the crystal's smooth surface. "I'll protect you," she whispered. "No matter what."

The crystal pulsed in response, a soft glow emanating from its core. Lena knew that her journey was far from over. There would be more challenges, more threats. But she was ready.

She was no longer just a girl with a dream. She was the Guardian of Time. And she would fulfill her destiny, no matter the cost.

The Aftermath

The chamber grew silent, the echoes of the confrontation fading into the ancient stone walls. Lena remained on her knees, her breathing shallow as the enormity of what had just happened settled over her. The crystal, its light now soft and steady, seemed to watch her, its pulse syncing with her own as if to reassure her that she had done the right thing.

For a fleeting moment, she allowed herself to feel relief. Montgomery and his men were gone—banished by the crystal's overwhelming power. But Lena knew that this was not the end. The crystal's energy carried a message, a warning. There would be more who sought its power, and their resolve might be far greater than Montgomery's.

She stood slowly, her legs shaky from the adrenaline and the energy she had expended. Her hand brushed the Talisman at her neck, the connection between her and the crystal now stronger than ever. It was her anchor, a reminder of her purpose. She had been chosen, not because she was powerful, but because she understood the delicate balance the crystal maintained.

New Understanding

Lena walked the perimeter of the chamber, her fingers trailing along the intricate carvings on the walls. The symbols told stories she could almost understand, fragments of a lost language that resonated deep within her. As she studied them, the crystal's hum seemed to grow louder, as if it were guiding her.

One set of symbols caught her attention—a series of concentric circles surrounding a figure standing at the center. Time radiated outward like ripples in a pond, and Lena realized with a jolt that the figure resembled her. Or perhaps, it represented all the guardians who had come before her.

The crystal wasn't just a key or a weapon; it was a bridge, a nexus between the past, present, and a future we could only see. The ancient civilization that had created it had understood its potential and its dangers. They had left these carvings as a guide for the one who would inherit the burden of its power.

The Talisman around her neck began to glow faintly, and Lena felt a tug in her chest—a pull toward the crystal. She approached it once more, her hand hesitating before she placed it on the cool, smooth surface. This time, the connection was immediate and overwhelming.

A Vision of the Past

The chamber faded, replaced by a landscape Lena had never seen before. She stood in a vast city of shimmering crystals, towers stretching toward a sky painted in hues of gold and violet. The hum of the crystal clock was everywhere, a constant rhythm that seemed to sustain the city itself.

People moved gracefully through the streets, their robes glinting in the light. They spoke a language Lena didn't recognize but somehow understood. These were the creators of the crystal clock, the ancient civilization that had unlocked the secrets of time. They had built their world around the crystal's energy, thriving in harmony with its power.

But the vision shifted.

The city darkened, its shimmering beauty replaced by chaos. The crystal clock, once a symbol of balance, now pulsed with an erratic, angry light. The people were divided—some sought to harness its power for personal gain, while others fought to protect it. The balance had been lost, and time itself began to fracture.

The vision ended abruptly, and Lena was back in the chamber, her hand still on the crystal. She staggered, the weight of what she had seen pressing down on her. The ancient civilization had fallen because they had misused the crystal's power. They had tried to control time, to bend it to their will, and they had paid the ultimate price.

She would not let history repeat itself.

A Guardian's Resolve

The air in the chamber felt charged, as if the crystal itself had shared its memories with Lena to prepare her for what lay ahead. She looked at it with new understanding, no longer seeing it as an artifact or a relic but as a living entity—a force that connected everything.

The Talisman grew warm against her skin, and Lena felt a renewed sense of purpose. She had been chosen not just to guard the crystal but to learn from it, to understand the delicate balance it maintained. The power it offered wasn't hers to wield freely— it was hers to protect, to ensure that it remained a force for balance rather than chaos.

She turned back toward the exit of the chamber, her footsteps steady despite the turmoil in her mind. Could Montgomery and his men somehow return, and others would surely come. But Lena wasn't the same person who had entered this temple. She had faced the crystal's power, felt its energy, and survived. She was stronger now, and she was ready for whatever came next.

A Warning from the Shadows

As Lena stepped into the light of the jungle, the humid air wrapping around her like a blanket, she felt a presence. She paused, her senses on high alert. The jungle was alive with sound, but this was different. She turned slowly, her hand instinctively moving to the Talisman.

A figure emerged from the shadows—a woman, cloaked in dark fabric that seemed to blend with the jungle itself. Her eyes gleamed with a strange light, and her movements were smooth, deliberate.

"You've done well," the woman said, her voice low and melodic. "But your journey is far from over."

Lena tensed, unsure whether this newcomer was friend or foe. "Who are you?" she asked, her voice firm.

The woman smiled faintly. "I am someone who has walked a similar path. The crystal chose you, as it once chose me. But be warned, guardian. The balance you seek to protect is more fragile than you realize. And the forces that oppose you are more powerful than you can imagine."

Lena narrowed her eyes. "What do you mean?"

"You've seen the visions," the woman said, stepping closer. "The fall of the ancient civilization was just the beginning. The crystal is not the only artifact of its kind. There are others— hidden, lost, waiting to be found. Together, they form the foundation of time itself. And if even one falls into the wrong hands..."

The woman let the sentence hang, the weight of her words sinking in.

"Then what do I do?" Lena asked, her voice barely above a whisper. "How do I stop it?"

The woman reached out, placing a hand over the Talisman. "You listen. The crystal will guide you, but you must be willing to sacrifice everything to protect it. The road ahead will be dangerous, and you will face choices that will test your very soul. But remember this: you are not alone."

With that, the woman turned and disappeared into thin air, her presence fading like a shadow.

A New Chapter

Lena stood in silence, the woman's words echoing in her mind. The crystal wasn't just a key or a weapon—it was part of something far greater. And her role as its guardian was just beginning.

She tightened her grip on the Talisman and turned back toward the jungle. The path ahead was uncertain, but Lena felt a strange sense of calm. She didn't have all the answers, but she had the crystal, the Talisman, and the strength to face whatever came next.

The power within her was no longer something to fear. It was her purpose. And she was ready to embrace it.

As she walked into the dense jungle to return to her camp and her team, the crystal's hum echoed in her heart, a constant reminder of the responsibility she now carried. The future is written with time, and Lena was determined to protect the balance of time, no matter what it took.

Chapter 17: The Collapse

The sky above the Andes churned with an eerie vibrancy, the kind that blurred the line between storm clouds and rips in the very fabric of existence. Lena stumbled over the rocky path leading from the temple, her breaths ragged and shallow as her surroundings twisted unnaturally. The once-stable world now shimmered like a mirage and a loom on the horizon, the air thick with a suffocating energy.

The crystal's dissonance pulsed through her veins, louder now, an urgent warning she could no longer ignore. Time itself was unraveling, its delicate threads torn apart by the power she had dared to wield. Every step she took felt heavier, the ground beneath her feet unstable, as though reality was buckling under her weight.

Her mind raced with memories—disjointed and overlapping. She saw flashes of her past, distorted by the ripple effects of her actions. The moment she had rewritten her team's perspective in the temple played over and over again, each time twisting into something more ominous. Faces shifted, voices blurred. Time wasn't linear anymore—it was folding in on itself.

She clutched the Talisman hanging from her neck, its faint glow the only thing grounding her in the chaos. The Shaman's voice echoed in her mind: **"You are the key. But even a key must tread lightly when opening the doors of time."**

The thought chilled her. The few changes that she had made, had she gone too far? This was a testament to times she had misused her power. Her gift.

Chapter 18: The Journey to the Shaman

Lena pushed forward, her pace quickening as the path narrowed into dense jungle. The village lay miles ahead, but it felt as if the distance expanded with every step. She could sense the collapse intensifying around her. Trees shifted in and out of focus, their outlines blurring like a poorly tuned frequency. The calls of wildlife echoed unnaturally, as if they were coming from another time entirely.

She paused to catch her breath, leaning against a jagged rock. The Talisman throbbed against her chest, urging her onward.

"Keep moving," she whispered to herself, her voice trembling. "You can fix this."

But could she? The weight of her failure bore down on her like an avalanche. She had thought she could control time, that her connection to the crystal was enough to manage its power. Now, she wasn't so sure. Every step she had taken in her journey—every experiment, every decision—had been a gamble. And now, the stakes were higher than she ever imagined.

The path ahead twisted violently, splitting into two directions. She stopped, her heart pounding. This had to be another distortion. She had walked this route many times; there was no fork here.

The jungle around her seemed to hold its breath, waiting for her choice.

A Glimpse of the Future

The sky above the Andes churned with an eerie vibrancy, the kind that blurred the line between storm clouds and rips in the very fabric of existence. Lena stumbled over the rocky path leading from the temple.

In a vision-Lena was older, her face worn and tired, her eyes hollow. She stood at the ruins of the temple, holding the Talisman in trembling hands. Around her were others—figures Lena didn't recognize, but their presence radiated menace. They circled her, their voices distorted and cruel, demanding answers, power, control.

"You failed," one of them hissed, its voice echoing like shattered glass. "Time belongs to no one."

Lena gasped, her heart pounding as the vision dissolved. She was back in the jungle, the path ahead of her once again clear. The Talisman's glow dimmed, but its warning lingered.

If she didn't act now, that vision would become her reality.

She clutched the Talisman hanging from her neck, its faint glow the only thing grounding her in the chaos. The Shaman's voice echoed in her mind: **"You are the key. But even a key must tread lightly when opening the doors of time."**

The thought chilled her. The few changes that she had made, had she gone too far? This was a testament to times she had misused her power. Her gift.

The Journey to the Shaman

Lena paced the edge of the encampment, her frustration bubbling beneath the surface. The crystal, once a source of guidance and clarity, now seemed distant and enigmatic. Its once-vivid glow had dimmed, and the hum that resonated within her chest was no longer steady—it wavered, erratic and confusing. Every attempt to connect with it left her feeling more disoriented, as if the answers she sought were buried beneath layers of uncertainty.

Her mind churned with questions that refused to settle. Why had the crystal brought her here if it wasn't going to guide her? What was she supposed to do next? The weight of her team's expectations and the growing tension among them only added to her turmoil. She felt trapped in a spiral of indecision, and the pressure was becoming unbearable.

Lena's thoughts turned to the Shaman. There was something about his presence—calm, grounded, and knowing—that seemed to cut through the noise. He had spoken in riddles, yes, but there was a wisdom in his words, a sense that he understood things that others could not. If anyone could help her make sense of the crystal's silence, it was him.

Without a second thought, Lena grabbed her notebook and the talisman that had grown faintly warm in her pocket. She slipped it into her palm, the familiar weight comforting against her skin. Determined, she made her way through the winding paths of the village, the setting sun casting long shadows over the stone streets. Her steps quickened as she neared the Shaman's modest hut, a small structure nestled against the curve of the mountainside.

She hesitated for a moment outside the doorway, the faint sound of wind chimes and the distant rustle of leaves filling the air. Taking a deep breath, she pushed the woven curtain aside and stepped inside. The space smelled of herbs and earth, the air thick with incense. The Shaman sat cross-legged in the center, his eyes closed, as though he had been expecting her.

"Child," he said without looking up, his voice low and steady. "You seek guidance once again."

Lena nodded, her voice trembling with frustration and urgency. "The crystal… it's not giving me anything. Everything feels wrong, chaotic. I don't know what to do, and I thought… maybe you could help me understand."

The Shaman opened his eyes, his gaze piercing yet kind. He gestured for her to sit across from him. "The crystal does not fail to guide you, Lena. It is you who must learn to listen in a different way."

His words only deepened her confusion, and she shook her head. "I've been trying! I've listened, meditated, focused… but nothing is clear. It's like it's shutting me out."

The Shaman reached for a small bowl of water beside him, dipping his fingers into it and letting the droplets fall onto the dirt floor. "The crystal is a mirror, reflecting your inner state. If the waters of your soul are turbulent, the reflection will be distorted. You must find stillness within yourself before you can hear what it has to say."

Lena clenched the talisman tighter, its warmth faint but persistent. "How am I supposed to do that when everything feels so… heavy? Everyone is counting on me. I don't have time to sit still."

The Shaman smiled faintly, as though he had heard these words countless times before. "The greatest journeys are not made with haste, child. Stillness is not the absence of action—it is the space in which clarity arises. If you cannot quiet the storm within, you will only hear echoes of your own doubt."

His words hung in the air, sinking into Lena's mind like seeds waiting to take root. For the first time, she felt a flicker of understanding. Perhaps it wasn't the crystal that had gone silent—it was her own inner turmoil drowning out its voice.

The Shaman reached out, placing his hand lightly over hers, where the talisman rested. "Go to the place where the sun meets the stone, as your dreams have shown you. Let the crystal speak, but let it speak through your heart, not your mind. Only then will its guidance become clear. If you succeed here, you must return to your Crystal immediately upon your return. You will know what to do."

Lena stared at him, her frustration softening into determination. The answer wasn't something she could force; it was something she had to allow. Nodding slowly, she rose to her feet, the talisman pulsing faintly in her grasp.

"Thank you," she said, her voice quieter now. The Shaman inclined his head, his expression unreadable.

As Lena stepped back out into the evening light, the hum in her chest steadied, a faint rhythm that seemed to echo the Shaman's words. She didn't have all the answers yet, but she knew where to begin. The path was hers to walk, and she would face it with the stillness she now understood she needed to find.

Into the Rift

The Shaman led Lena to the outskirts of the village, where the jungle gave way to an open clearing. In the center of the clearing was a swirling vortex of light and shadow—a tear in reality, a rift where time itself bled into the physical world.

"This is where it begins," the Shaman said, his voice solemn. "The crystal's energy is tied to this rift. If you step through, you will face the consequences of your actions. You will see what you have done, and you will be given a choice. But be warned, Lena—what lies beyond the rift is not bound by the rules of our world."

Lena stared at the rift, her body trembling. She could feel its pull, its chaotic energy tugging at her very soul. She wanted to run, to turn away and forget everything. But she couldn't. The visions, the collapse, the destruction—she had caused this, and she had to fix it if she could.

"I'm ready," she said, her voice steady despite the fear gnawing at her chest.

The Shaman nodded, his expression softening. "Then go, Guardian of Time. Face the power within."

Lena stepped into the rift.

A World Unmade

The moment she crossed the threshold, the air around her shifted. She was no longer in the jungle. She stood in a vast, empty expanse, the ground beneath her feet shimmering like liquid glass. Above her, the sky was a chaotic swirl of light and darkness, the fractures of time stretching infinitely in every direction.

Lena turned slowly, her heart pounding. In the distance, she saw a figure—a reflection of herself, standing still, waiting. The reflection smiled, but it wasn't a kind smile. It was cold, calculating.

"You think you can fix this?" the reflection said, its voice a perfect mimicry of Lena's own. "You think you can undo what you've done?"

Lena stepped closer, her fists clenched. "I have to try."

The reflection laughed, a sound that sent shivers down her spine. "The crystal doesn't need you. It never did. You're just a vessel, a pawn. Do you really believe you're in control?"

Lena's anger flared. "I'm not a pawn. I'm the Guardian of Time. And I will protect it."

The reflection's smile faded. "Then prove it."

The ground beneath them shifted, and Lena found herself surrounded by fragments of her past—moments she had altered, choices she had made. The weight of her actions pressed down on her, but she stood tall.

"I'll prove it," Lena said, her voice unwavering. "No matter what it takes."

As the reflection dissolved into the swirling chaos, Lena stepped forward, ready to face whatever the crystal demanded of her.

And this time, she would not fail.

The Test of the Guardian

The obelisk split into three sections, each forming a distinct portal. Through the first, Lena saw a vision of the past—the ancient civilization that had created the Crystal Clock. She saw their rituals, their discoveries, their desperate attempts to harness time's power. It was beautiful and terrible all at once.

Through the second portal, she saw the present—her team in the jungle, searching for her. Montgomery was rallying the others, their intentions unclear but undeniably dangerous. If she did nothing, they would find the crystal, and its power would fall into the wrong hands.

The third portal revealed the future—a fractured, apocalyptic world. The sky was torn, time itself unraveling into chaos. She saw herself standing amidst the ruins, older and broken, touching the crystal as the last threads of existence dissolved around her.

"These are your paths," the Voice said. "The past, the present, and the future. Each demands your intervention, but you may choose only one. The Balance cannot be restored without sacrifice."

Lena's breath hitched. "I have to choose? But—what happens to the other two paths if I don't choose them?"

"They will remain as they are, broken and unhealed. Your choice will define the course of time, but it will also leave scars."

Lena's mind raced. The past called to her, offering a chance to understand the origins of the crystal and prevent the ancient civilization's downfall. But the present demanded action—her team was in danger, and the crystal needed protection. And the future... how could she ignore the devastation she had seen?

She clenched her fists, the Talisman pulsing in her grasp. "How do I know what the right choice is?"

"There is no right choice, Guardian," the Voice said. "Only the one you are willing to live with."

Choosing a Path

Lena's gaze flicked between the portals, her heart pounding in her chest. She thought of everything she had learned, everything she had sacrificed. The crystal had chosen her, but now, it was her turn to choose.

She stepped toward the second portal—the present.

"I can't ignore what's happening now," she said, her voice steady. "If I don't stop them, the crystal will fall into the wrong hands, and everything will spiral out of control."

The Voice seemed to nod, though Lena couldn't see it. "Very well. But know this, Guardian—by choosing the present, you forfeit the chance to rewrite the past or secure the future. The consequences of your choice will ripple through time."

"I understand," Lena said, though her stomach churned with doubt.

The portal flared, engulfing her in a blinding light.

Confronting the Present

Lena stumbled as she emerged from the portal, back in the jungle outside the temple in a moment of time when she was about to be confronted by Montgomery. The air was thick with tension, the sounds of Montgomery's team growing louder. She clutched the Talisman tightly, feeling its power resonate with the crystal deep within the temple.

She had one chance to stop them.

Montgomery appeared first, his eyes narrowing as he spotted her. "Lena," he said, his tone a mixture of surprise and triumph. "I knew you'd come back."

"I can't let you take the crystal," Lena said, her voice firm. "You don't understand what you're dealing with."

Montgomery sneered. "And you do? This power is bigger than you, Lena. It's bigger than all of us. You think you can control it, but you're wrong. The crystal doesn't belong to you."

"It doesn't belong to anyone," Lena shot back. "It's not meant to be used as a weapon."

The rest of the team emerged from the shadows, their faces filled with uncertainty. Some looking for guidance, while others seemed torn, as if questioning their own motives.

Lena took a deep breath, feeling the crystal's energy surge within her. "I don't want to hurt anyone," she said. "But if you try to use the crystal, I will stop you."

Montgomery's expression darkened. "You don't have the power to stop me."

But Lena did. She felt it coursing through her, a steady, unyielding force. Time itself bent to her will, and as she raised her hand, the jungle seemed to still. Leaves froze mid-fall, the air grew heavy, and the world became quiet.

"I do," she said, her voice resonating with the crystal's hum. "And I will."

Restoring the Balance

The confrontation was over before it began. Lena didn't need to fight. She let the crystal's energy speak for her, its light overwhelming the jungle. The others fell back, their weapons dropping as they shielded their eyes.

Montgomery stared at her, his confidence crumbling. "What... what are you?"

"I'm the Guardian," Lena said. "And this ends now."

With a final surge of power, she pushed them back, time shifting around her to ensure their retreat. When the light faded, she stood alone, the crystal safe once more.

But the balance had been restored at a cost. The portals were gone, the past and future locked away. Lena felt the weight of her choice settle in her chest. She had saved the present, but the scars of her actions would remain.

When Lena exited the portal, the mountain path was eerily silent, the occasional rustle of leaves the only sound breaking the oppressive quiet. Lena tightened the straps of her bag, her boots crunching against the loose gravel. The ascent was steep and treacherous, but it mirrored the turmoil within her. She had met the Shaman only hours ago, and his words still echoed in her mind like a warning bell.

"You have tampered with forces older than the stars," the Shaman had said, his weathered hands clasping hers with surprising strength. *"The Crystal Clock is a guardian, not a tool. You must return to where it all began and make things right. If you fail, time will devour itself."*

The idea of time being "devoured" had haunted her since. She couldn't quite visualize what the Shaman meant, but she didn't need to. She had felt it—the fractures, the instability, the way reality itself seemed to warp and shift unpredictably. Time wasn't just moving forward anymore; it was unraveling. Lena had made mistakes, yes, but she hadn't realized how deep the consequences ran until now.

The cave was her only hope. It was where her dreams had begun, where her connection to the crystal had first been forged. If there was any place to repair what she had broken, it was there.

As she stood in the quiet of the jungle, the Talisman glowing faintly against her skin, Lena knew her journey was far from over. The crystal was safe at the moment, but the Balance would always need protecting now.

The Path of Memory

As she climbed higher into the mountains, Lena's mind replayed the events that had led her here. Her first encounter with the Crystal Clock flashed vividly—its hum, its light, the inexplicable pull that had drawn her to it like a moth to a flame. She had thought it was a gift, a revelation meant for her to explore. But the Shaman's scolding had made her see it differently. It wasn't hers. It was a force far greater than her understanding, something ancient and untamed.

Lena's thoughts drifted to her choices: stopping time, bending it, changing small things she thought wouldn't matter. She had meant no harm, but her actions had rippled outward, affecting people and events in ways she hadn't anticipated. She had turned Montgomery's ambition into desperation, shifted the lives of her team, and—perhaps worst of all—had fractured the delicate balance that kept time itself stable.

The wind picked up as she neared the entrance to the cave. The hum began, faint at first but growing louder with every step. Lena's heartbeat quickened. The air around her seemed to vibrate, charged with an energy that made her hair stand on end. She tightened her grip on the Talisman around her neck, its surface warm against her skin.

The open cave loomed ahead, its mouth a dark void against the craggy rock. It was as if the mountain itself was holding its breath, waiting for her to step inside.

The Cave's Whisper

The moment Lena entered the cave, the hum enveloped her. It wasn't just a sound—it was a presence, an energy that seeped into her very bones. The air was heavy, as though it carried the weight of millennia. The walls shimmered faintly, glowing with the same blue light as the crystal deeper within. The energy was different this time—erratic, unstable. The crystal wasn't just calling to her; it was crying out for help.

She moved cautiously through the winding passage, her footsteps echoing softly. Every inch of the cave felt alive, pulsating with the power of the Crystal Clock. As she approached the central chamber, Lena's breath caught. There it was.

The crystal stood tall and majestic, its surface fractured with jagged lines of light that pulsed erratically. It looked as though it were struggling to hold itself together, its energy spilling out in chaotic waves. Lena felt a pang of guilt. This was her doing. She had disrupted its balance, and now it was breaking apart.

She stepped closer, her hand instinctively reaching out to touch the crystal. But before her fingers could make contact, a wave of energy surged outward, knocking her back. She stumbled, falling to her knees, the Talisman glowing brightly against her chest.

"You have come."

The voice was not human. It was deep, resonant, vibrating through the chamber. Lena's eyes darted around, but she saw no one. The voice seemed to emanate from the crystal itself.

"I didn't mean for this to happen," Lena said, her voice trembling. "I didn't understand what I was doing."

"Intentions mean nothing to time," the voice replied. *"Only actions."*

Lena felt tears welling up. "I want to fix it. Tell me what to do. Please."

The crystal's light dimmed for a moment, and the voice softened. *"To restore balance, you must let go. The power you seek to control is not yours. It is a force that must remain unclaimed, untamed. Only then can the flow of time be made whole."*

The Ritual

Lena took a deep breath, steadying herself. The Shaman's words echoed in her mind: *"You will know what to do when the moment comes."* She reached for the Talisman, the one thing that had tied her to the crystal since the beginning. Its energy pulsed in sync with the crystal's, a connection she now realized was the key to everything.

Closing her eyes, she focused on the rhythm—the hum of the crystal, the thrum of the Talisman, the beating of her own heart. Slowly, she raised the Talisman, holding it aloft. The crystal responded immediately, its light flaring brighter as if recognizing her intention.

The words came to her unbidden, ancient syllables that resonated deep within her soul. She spoke them aloud, her voice growing stronger with each repetition. The chamber vibrated, the walls shimmering as the energy within the crystal began to stabilize.

The light from the Talisman merged with the crystal's glow, creating a cascade of colors that filled the chamber. Lena felt the energy flow through her, a powerful current that seemed to strip away her fears, her doubts. She was no longer just Lena. She was a conduit, a vessel for the crystal's energy.

As the chant reached its crescendo, the ground beneath her feet trembled. The crystal began to sink into the earth, its light dimming as it receded. Lena continued the ritual, her voice unwavering, even as the cave began to shake.

The Collapse

The moment the crystal disappeared completely, the cave began to crumble. Rocks fell from the ceiling, and the ground split beneath her. Lena turned and ran, the Talisman still glowing faintly around her neck. The passage narrowed as she sprinted, her lungs burning, her legs screaming for rest.

Just as she reached the cave's mouth, the entrance collapsed behind her with a deafening roar. She stumbled into the open air, falling to her knees as dust and debris billowed out around her. The mountain seemed to sigh, the vibrations fading into silence.

Lena sat there, her breath coming in ragged gasps. It was done. The crystal was sealed, hidden away where no one could reach it. She had restored the balance—at least, she hoped she had.

A New Beginning

As the sun began to rise over the mountains, Lena felt a sense of peace wash over her. The Talisman around her neck was cool now, its glow faint but steady. She didn't know what the future held, but she knew one thing for certain: the crystal was no longer her burden to bear.

The Shaman's words came back to her: *"You are a guardian, Lena. But even guardians must know when to step back."*

She stood, brushing the dirt from her clothes, and looked out over the jungle below. The world felt... different. Lighter. The fractures in time had healed, the chaos dissipated. For the first time in what felt like forever, the air was still.

Lena turned and began the long trek down the mountain, a faint smile on her lips. The journey was over, but her story was far from finished. Time had tested her, broken her, and rebuilt her. She was stronger now, wiser. And though the crystal was gone, its lessons would stay with her forever.

She had returned the crystal to the earth. She had restored the Balance. And now, she was ready to face whatever came next.

A World Renewed

Lena's descent down the mountain was filled with a strange stillness, the kind that didn't come from the absence of sound but from the presence of balance. The world felt recalibrated. Each step she took was lighter, the burden she had carried for so long finally lifted. She no longer felt the hum of the crystal pulling at her chest or the dissonance of fractured timelines clouding her mind.

The jungle below looked alive in a way she hadn't noticed before—vibrant greens shimmering under the soft glow of the rising sun, the sound of birds filling the air in harmonious rhythm. It was as if the universe itself had breathed a sigh of relief, settling into the natural flow of time once more.

But Lena wasn't naïve. She knew her actions, while monumental, were not the end of the story. The Shaman had warned her that the balance of time was delicate, always teetering on the edge. And while the crystal was sealed, hidden away where it could no longer be misused, the knowledge of its existence—and the power it held—would remain in the minds of those who had sought it.

Her thoughts turned to the men who had chased her, their greed for power driving them to risk the very fabric of reality. She didn't know what had happened to them after the cave collapsed. Perhaps they had been caught in the destabilization of time, lost to the ripples of their own ambition. Or perhaps they were out there still, regrouping, plotting their next move.

Lena tightened her grip on the Talisman as it rested against her chest. It no longer radiated the overwhelming energy it once had, but its presence was still reassuring, a reminder of her role as a guardian. The Shaman had called it a symbol, a connection to something greater. And while Lena didn't fully understand the extent of its power, she knew it was a part of her now—just as the crystal had been.

Reuniting with the Team

By the time Lena reached the outskirts of the village, the sun was high in the sky, its golden rays casting a warm glow over the thatched rooftops and cobblestone paths. The villagers moved about their day with an ease that made Lena's heart ache with longing. She wanted that peace, that simplicity. But she also knew it wasn't her path—not yet.

The small research camp her team had set up was just beyond the village, nestled in a clearing surrounded by towering trees. As she approached, she could hear the murmur of voices, the clatter of equipment. It felt like a lifetime ago that she had been among them, driven by the thrill of discovery and the promise of answers.

When she stepped into the clearing, all movement ceased. The team turned to her, their expressions a mix of relief, confusion, and apprehension. Professor Ruiz was the first to approach, his face lined with worry.

"Lena," he said, his voice heavy with emotion. "We thought we'd lost you. After the cave... we didn't know if you—"

"I'm okay," she interrupted gently, her gaze meeting his. "The crystal is sealed. The cave collapsed. It's over."

Ruiz studied her for a long moment, his eyes searching hers for answers she wasn't ready to give. Finally, he nodded, his shoulders sagging with relief. "You did it," he said, though his tone carried an undercurrent of disbelief. "You actually did it."

The rest of the team began to gather around, their questions coming in a flurry. What had happened in the cave? What had caused the collapse? Was the crystal truly gone?

Lena raised a hand, silencing them. "The crystal's power was too great," she said simply. "It had to be hidden, protected. No one can use it now—not for good, not for harm."

Her words hung in the air, met with a mix of acceptance and doubt. She knew they wouldn't fully understand—how could they? They hadn't seen what she had, hadn't felt the raw energy of time itself unraveling. But they didn't need to understand. All they needed to know was that the danger had passed.

A Warning Unheeded

As the camp settled into an uneasy calm, Lena found herself standing on the edge of the clearing, gazing out at the dense jungle. She couldn't shake the feeling that her journey wasn't truly over. The crystal was hidden, yes, but it wasn't destroyed. Its power still existed, waiting, and there would always be those who sought to claim it.

"Do you think it's really over?" Ruiz's voice broke the silence, and Lena turned to see him standing beside her, his arms crossed.

"For now," she said quietly. "But people like Montgomery... they don't just give up. They'll come back. Maybe not for this crystal, but for something else. The desire for power doesn't die easily."

Ruiz nodded, his expression grim. "What about you? What's next?"

Lena considered his question. She had spent so much time chasing the answers the crystal seemed to promise, so much time caught in the pull of its energy. Now that it was gone, she wasn't sure what came next. But one thing was clear—her role as a guardian wasn't over.

"I'll keep moving forward," she said finally. "The Shaman told me the balance of time is fragile. It's not just about the crystal. It's about understanding how everything is connected—how every action ripples outward. I need to keep learning, keep protecting."

Ruiz tilted his head, a faint smile tugging at the corners of his mouth. "You've changed, Lena. You're not the same person who walked into that cave four weeks ago."

Lena returned his smile, though it was tinged with sadness. "None of us are."

The Weight of Responsibility

That night, as the camp settled into a restless sleep, Lena sat by the fire, the Talisman clutched tightly in her hand. She thought about the Shaman's final words to her, spoken just before she left the village.

"You are part of the balance now, Lena. The choices you make will shape more than just your own path. They will shape the flow of time itself. Trust your instincts, but never forget the cost of power."

The weight of those words pressed heavily on her, but she welcomed it. She had seen the cost of misuse, the devastation that could follow even the smallest shift in time. And she had learned to respect the power she carried—not as something to be wielded, but as something to protect.

As the fire crackled softly, Lena looked up at the night sky, the stars scattered like fragments of time itself. She felt a strange sense of peace, knowing that the crystal was safe, hidden from those who would exploit it. But she also felt the stirrings of something greater—a purpose that stretched far beyond what she had imagined.

The world had been changed by her actions, and Lena knew she couldn't return to the life she had known before. But she didn't want to. She had a new path now, one that would take her to places she couldn't yet foresee.

For the first time in a long while, Lena allowed herself to hope. The journey ahead would be difficult, but it would also be hers. And she was ready.

Chapter 19: A New Beginning

The air was thick with the scent of earth and the crisp bite of mountain wind as Lena descended from the now-sealed cave. The energy that had once thrummed through her veins was absent, leaving her feeling lighter but oddly hollow. She paused on a jagged outcropping, gazing at the mountain she had just left behind. Its jagged peaks stretched skyward, their silent majesty belying the ancient power now entombed within.

The Crystal Clock was gone from her grasp, hidden beneath layers of rock and time itself. For a fleeting moment, she touched the pendant resting against her chest—the Talisman that had once pulsed in harmony with the crystal. Now, it was little more than a cold weight. The hum that had guided her for so long was gone, leaving behind a silence that pressed on her mind like a heavy shroud.

Yet, as Lena stood there, the enormity of what she had accomplished began to settle over her. She had saved the world—or so she believed. The timeline was stable again, the fractures she had caused mended. Time, in all its fluid, unyielding complexity, was moving forward without interference. The crystal was no longer a tool for manipulation, no longer a temptation for those who sought to control reality itself.

But even as she tried to embrace this victory, doubt crept into her heart.

The Emptiness of Resolution

Back at camp, the world felt strangely mundane. The researchers bustled around her, packing equipment, cataloging artifacts, and preparing for their journey home. Their excitement about the expedition seemed almost trivial in light of what Lena had faced. They had no idea of the danger that had loomed over them, of how close the world had come to unraveling.

Professor Ruiz approached her, his face a mask of quiet concern. He had been uncharacteristically subdued since their escape from the cave. Perhaps he had seen enough in those final moments to understand that something extraordinary had occurred—something that defied explanation.

"You've been quiet," Ruiz said, his voice low as he sat beside her on a fallen log. "I can't imagine what you've been through. But you did it. The crystal is gone, and we're all safe because of you."

Lena nodded but didn't look at him. Her eyes remained fixed on the horizon, where the sun was beginning its slow descent. "Safe," she murmured. The word felt fragile, like a promise she wasn't sure she could keep.

Ruiz leaned forward, his elbows resting on his knees. "What's on your mind?"

She hesitated. How could she explain the weight of what she had experienced? The hum of the crystal had been more than a guide—it had been a part of her, a connection to something far greater than herself. Now that it was gone, she felt unmoored, like a ship adrift without a compass.

"It's quiet now," she said finally. "Too quiet."

Ruiz frowned. "The crystal?"

Lena nodded. "For as long as I can remember, it's been there—guiding me, calling to me. Even before I knew what it was, I could feel it. And now… it's gone."

"That's a good thing, isn't it?" Ruiz asked cautiously. "You've done what you needed to do. The crystal's power can't hurt anyone anymore."

"Maybe," Lena said. "But it was more than just power. It was knowledge. Connection. Purpose. Without it…" She trailed off, unsure how to put her feelings into words.

Ruiz placed a reassuring hand on her shoulder. "You've protected the world from something unimaginable. That's no small thing, Lena. And maybe now, you can finally rest."

The Ripple Effect

Rest. The word lingered in Lena's mind as the camp settled into its final night. The researchers would leave in the morning, their work here complete. But Lena wasn't sure she was ready to go. The mountain, the jungle, even the lingering echoes of the crystal's energy—they felt like unfinished chapters in a story she couldn't yet close.

As the campfire crackled and the team shared quiet conversations, Lena wandered to the edge of the clearing. The jungle beyond was alive with sound—the chirping of crickets, the rustle of leaves in the wind. Yet, beneath it all, there was a stillness, a faint sense of imbalance that she couldn't shake.

She had fixed the fractures in time—or so she believed. But time was a delicate thing, a web of interwoven threads. Even the smallest disruption could send ripples through the entire structure, ripples that might not reveal their consequences for years, or even centuries. Had she truly repaired the damage, or had she merely delayed the inevitable?

Her thoughts drifted to the Shaman's words: *"The balance of time is never guaranteed. It must be guarded, always."* She had thought sealing the crystal would be enough, but now she wasn't so sure.

Lena's gaze fell to the Talisman around her neck. Its once-vibrant glow had faded, but it still held a faint warmth, as if it were waiting. For what, she didn't know.

A Flicker in the Darkness

The next morning, the team began their journey back to civilization. Lena walked with them, but her mind was elsewhere. The path through the jungle was treacherous, the terrain uneven and the air thick with humidity. Yet, the challenge of the journey felt almost comforting—a distraction from the gnawing emptiness inside her.

As they neared the edge of the jungle, Lena felt it again—a faint ripple in the air, like a shift in the wind that didn't belong. She stopped in her tracks, her hand instinctively reaching for the Talisman. It vibrated faintly against her skin, and for a moment, she felt the hum again—not as strong as before, but unmistakable.

She turned, her eyes scanning the jungle behind her. The others continued walking, their voices fading into the distance. But Lena remained rooted to the spot, her breath caught in her throat.

And then she saw it.

A faint shimmer, barely visible against the dense greenery, like a mirage flickering in and out of existence. It was the same distortion she had seen from the mountain—a ripple in the fabric of reality. Time itself, bending.

Her heart raced. The crystal was sealed, its power contained. But this… this was something else.

A Choice to Make

Lena stood frozen, torn between two worlds. She could follow the team, return to the life she had known before all of this began. Or she could step into the unknown once more, pursue the mystery that called to her, even if it meant risking everything.

The shimmer grew stronger, its edges pulsing with light. It wasn't just a ripple—it was an opening. A door to somewhere—somewhere—else.

Lena took a deep breath, the weight of the Talisman pressing against her chest. The Shaman's words echoed in her mind: *"The choices you make will shape more than just your own path. They will shape the flow of time itself."*

This was her choice. Her responsibility. And as much as she wanted to walk away, to leave the crystal and its power behind, she knew she couldn't. The ripple was a sign, a call to action. The balance of time wasn't guaranteed. It had to be guarded.

Lena turned away from the team and stepped toward the shimmer. With each step, the world around her seemed to fade, the jungle dissolving into a haze of light. The air grew colder, the hum of the Talisman growing louder.

And then, with a final step, she crossed the threshold.

Into the Unknown

The world on the other side was unlike anything Lena had ever seen. It was a place of endless light and shadow, where time seemed to flow in every direction at once. She felt weightless, untethered, as if she were floating between moments. The hum of the Talisman was deafening now, resonating with the very fabric of this strange realm.

Lena didn't know where she was, or what she was meant to do. But as she stood there, suspended in the flow of time itself, one thing became clear.

Her journey was far from over.

Stepping Beyond Time

Lena drifted through the strange, luminous expanse, her senses overwhelmed by the sheer enormity of the place she had entered. The shimmer that had drawn her here was now gone, leaving her alone in what could only be described as the nexus of time itself. Light swirled in every direction, refracting like the facets of a crystal, but there was no discernible source. It felt infinite, both in space and possibility, but also eerily fragile, as if one wrong step could unravel the very fabric holding it all together.

The hum of the Talisman was her only anchor, vibrating steadily against her chest. It felt alive, like a compass guiding her forward through the intangible currents of the realm. The sound was no longer overwhelming, as it had been near the crystal—this hum was softer, steadier, as though it were attuned to her heartbeat. For the first time since entering the nexus, Lena felt a faint flicker of reassurance.

She extended her hand, and the swirling light around her reacted instantly, bending toward her fingers like liquid drawn to gravity. Her breath hitched. The realm wasn't just alive—it was responding to her presence, her movements, her intent. A small, cautious step forward sent ripples through the light, as if she were walking on the surface of a shimmering lake. Each ripple revealed glimpses of something beyond the immediate expanse: fleeting images of faces, landscapes, and moments that vanished as quickly as they appeared.

It wasn't random. These weren't just fragments of possibility—they were threads of time, lives and events woven into the tapestry of reality. And she was walking through it, a guardian within the intricate web of existence.

But if the nexus was a web, then something had left it frayed. Here and there, Lena could see dark tendrils snaking through the light, disrupting the flow. They pulsed and twisted unnaturally, like veins of decay spreading through the lifeblood of time itself. Wherever these shadows reached, the images flickered and dimmed, their vibrancy consumed by the encroaching void.

Her chest tightened. This wasn't just the aftermath of her actions—this was something more. Something deliberate.

The Keeper of the Threshold

"You've come."

The voice startled Lena, breaking the heavy silence of the nexus. It was deep, resonant, and carried a weight that seemed to echo beyond the limits of the realm. She turned sharply, her hand instinctively clutching the Talisman.

A figure emerged from the swirling light, its form shimmering as though it were made from the same essence as the nexus itself. The figure was tall, cloaked in an iridescent robe that seemed to shift between colors with every movement. Its face was obscured, as if light and shadow were battling for dominance across its features. Yet its eyes—piercing, unblinking—locked onto Lena with an intensity that rooted her to the spot.

"You've come far," the figure said, stepping closer. Its voice was neither male nor female, but carried the weight of countless lifetimes. "But your journey is far from over."

Lena swallowed hard, her mind racing. "Who are you? What is this place?"

The figure tilted its head, as though considering her carefully. "I am a Keeper. A sentinel of this realm. This is the Between—the confluence of all timelines, all possibilities. It is here that the threads of existence are woven and maintained."

Lena's gaze darted to the dark tendrils that continued to writhe through the light. "And those? What's happening to them?"

The Keeper's expression darkened. "An imbalance. A corruption spreading through the threads of time. It is not natural. It is not chaos. It is deliberate."

Lena's pulse quickened. "Deliberate? By who?"

The Keeper's eyes seemed to pierce deeper into her. "You already know."

The words struck her like a blow. She thought of the shadowy figures who had pursued her, the ones who had sought the crystal's power for themselves. But it wasn't just them. The Shaman's warnings echoed in her mind: *There are those who would twist time to their will, who see it not as a force to be respected but as a tool to be wielded.*

"Montgomery," Lena whispered, the name falling from her lips like a curse. The professor had been ambitious, driven by the desire to understand the crystal's power. But had his obsession driven him to this? Was he responsible for the corruption spreading through the threads of time?

The Keeper nodded. "He and others like him. They seek to control what cannot be controlled. They manipulate the threads for their own gain, unaware—or uncaring—of the destruction they leave in their wake."

Lena felt a surge of anger, but it was quickly tempered by guilt. She had also manipulated time, albeit with different intentions. Had her actions contributed to this imbalance? Was she just as culpable?

"Can it be fixed?" she asked, her voice trembling.

The Keeper's gaze softened, and for a moment, Lena thought she saw something human in its expression. "That depends on you. The crystal chose you not because of your power, but because of your understanding. You feel the flow of time as others cannot. You can restore what has been broken."

Lena's hand tightened around the Talisman. "What do I have to do?"

Weaving the Threads

The Keeper, Elira, extended its hand, and a glowing strand of light materialized in the air between them. Lena watched in awe as the strand unraveled into countless smaller threads, each one shimmering with a unique hue. Together, they formed a complex pattern—a tapestry of interwoven moments and possibilities.

"This is time," Elira said. "A living, breathing entity. To repair it, you must first understand it. Follow the threads. See where they lead. And find the source of the corruption."

Before Lena could respond, the Keeper touched her forehead with a single, glowing finger. A rush of energy coursed through her, and suddenly, she was no longer standing in the nexus.

She was moving.

Walking Through Time

The world around Lena blurred and shifted as she followed the threads of light. Each one pulled her into a different moment—a bustling marketplace in an ancient civilization, a quiet library filled with books from an unknown future, a battlefield where soldiers clashed under a crimson sky. Every moment felt real, vivid, as though she were truly there.

But the corruption was always present, a dark stain creeping into each scene. She saw it twist the actions of a king, turning a moment of peace into a declaration of war. She saw it infect a scientist's mind, driving them to create something monstrous. And she saw it touch ordinary people, turning acts of kindness into seeds of discord.

Each time, Lena reached out, her hands brushing against the threads of light. She willed them to heal, to return to their natural flow. The Talisman glowed brighter with each attempt, its energy intertwining with hers. Slowly, the darkness began to retreat, the threads restoring themselves to their original vibrancy.

But it wasn't enough.

The Final Thread

As Lena approached the final thread, she felt a familiar presence—one that made her blood run cold. Standing at the edge of the nexus, where the light met the void, was Montgomery.

He turned as she approached, his expression a mix of triumph and defiance. In his hand, he held a shard of the crystal, its fractured light casting eerie shadows across his face.

"You're too late, Lena," he said, his voice echoing unnaturally. "I've seen what this power can do. I can reshape everything—perfect the timeline."

"You're destroying it!" Lena shouted, her voice trembling with anger. "You're unraveling everything for your own selfish ambitions."

Montgomery sneered. "And what are you doing? Playing the hero? Don't pretend you're any different."

Lena stepped forward, her resolve hardening. "I made mistakes. But I'm here to fix them. Can you say the same?"

The two stood facing each other, the weight of the nexus pressing down on them. Lena knew this was the moment that would decide everything. The balance of time rested on her next move.

With a deep breath, she reached for the final thread.

Lena's hand hovered over the glowing strand, the Talisman pulsing with energy. The nexus trembled around her, the light and shadow locked in a battle that mirrored the one raging within her.

Lena was able to restore balance without losing herself in the process. She knew that only time itself had the answers of what lay ahead, just beyond the final thread.

Chapter 20: A New Journey Awaits

Suddenly, Lena stood motionless on the cliff's edge, the golden hues of the Andean sunset casting her shadow long and thin against the rocky ground. The winds tugged at her clothes, carrying with them the faint whispers of distant times, moments both past and yet to come. Her chest tightened as she replayed Elira's words in her mind, their weight heavy with an undeniable truth. The woman's piercing gaze, her ethereal presence, and the cryptic warning had shattered the fragile illusion that Lena's journey was over.

Far below, the jungle stretched endlessly, a sea of green and shadow. Yet, to Lena, it seemed less like a physical expanse and more like the surface of an uncharted map—an endless web of possibilities and dangers. The Talisman at her chest vibrated faintly, as if alive, attuned to the shifts in the fabric of reality. The hum that had been silent since her encounter with the crystal now resonated stronger, more intricate, and with it came a revelation: she wasn't just connected to the crystal. She was connected to the universe itself.

The Call of the Unknown

Lena turned away from the cliff's edge, her mind racing. The idea of forces beyond Earth vying for control of the crystal's power felt impossibly vast, yet Elira's warning had carried an undeniable certainty. The universe, once an abstract concept of stars and voids, now felt tangible, personal, alive. And it was watching her.

The Talisman pulsed again, pulling her attention downward. As she looked at the small, fused halves—the gift from Mrs. Harrison and the piece from the Shaman—Lena felt a strange shift in her perception. The world around her seemed to ripple, as if time itself were adjusting to her awareness. It wasn't a full disruption, like the fractures she had witnessed before, but a subtle acknowledgment that she was no longer bound by the same rules.

Her fingers tightened around the Talisman as the hum intensified. Suddenly, the air around her thickened, the horizon distorting as though it were bending inward. Lena stumbled, the world shifting beneath her feet. And then, just as quickly as it began, the distortion faded, leaving her standing in a different place entirely.

She was no longer on the cliff.

Between Realities

The space around Lena was indescribable—neither light nor dark, solid nor fluid. Colors and shapes shifted, undefined yet familiar, like half-remembered dreams. Time itself felt suspended, as if the seconds were stretching and contracting in an infinite dance.

Lena's heart raced as she looked around, her senses overwhelmed by the strangeness of the space. Yet amidst the chaos, she felt an odd calm. This wasn't a random event; it was the crystal—or rather, the Talisman—guiding her. She had crossed into the in-between, the fold of time and space Elira had alluded to.

As she moved forward, her footsteps creating faint ripples in the shifting ground, Lena began to see faint outlines—threads of light stretching across the expanse. They were familiar, reminiscent of the threads she had seen in the nexus of time. These were paths, connections to different moments, timelines, or perhaps even dimensions. Each thread pulsed with its own rhythm, its own story.

But not all of them glowed brightly. Among the vibrant strands were others, dark and frayed, their energy distorted and unnatural. Lena felt a chill as she approached one of these corrupted threads. The closer she got, the more she could feel the decay—an ache deep in her chest, as if the imbalance itself was reaching for her.

The Talisman grew warm against her skin, and instinctively, Lena reached out toward the thread. As her fingers brushed against its surface, a wave of images flooded her mind—moments of destruction, chaos, and despair. She saw figures she didn't recognize—some human, others distinctly not—wielding power that felt eerily familiar. They were manipulating the threads, bending time and reality for their own gain, and the ripple effects were devastating.

Lena pulled her hand back, her breath catching in her throat. Elira had been right. This wasn't just about the crystal. The forces she had glimpsed weren't bound by Earth's limitations; they operated on a cosmic scale, their ambitions stretching far beyond what Lena had imagined.

A New Purpose

The realization settled over Lena like a heavy weight, but with it came clarity. She wasn't just the guardian of the crystal—she was a guardian of time itself. The Talisman had chosen her not just to seal the crystal, but to act as a bridge between realities, a protector of the delicate balance that held the universe together.

The thought was overwhelming, but Lena didn't feel fear. She felt... ready.

The hum of the Talisman deepened, and Lena felt a new awareness awaken within her. She could feel the threads now, not just see them. She could sense their flow, their connections, their vulnerabilities. It was as if time itself was offering her a hand, showing her how to navigate its complexities without causing harm.

She reached out again, this time with purpose. Her fingers grazed a nearby thread, one that glowed faintly but seemed frayed at the edges. As she focused on it, she felt herself drawn into its flow, her consciousness merging with the moment it represented.

Suddenly, she was standing in a bustling marketplace, the air filled with the sounds of trade and laughter. The thread pulsed around her, and Lena realized she was witnessing a moment—a single point in time. She moved through the crowd, unnoticed, observing the flow of events. And then she saw it—a shadowy figure slipping through the crowd, its hand reaching for an object that glowed faintly in its grasp.

It was a shard of the crystal.

Lena's heart raced as she watched the figure disappear into the crowd. This was one of the forces Elira had warned her about, a being capable of crossing between worlds to claim the crystal's power. But as Lena moved to follow, she felt the thread begin to unravel. The moment was fragile, teetering on the edge of collapse.

She stepped back, her instincts telling her not to intervene. Instead, she focused on the thread itself, using the Talisman to stabilize it. The frayed edges began to mend, the moment solidifying once more. The shadowy figure faded, the presence erased as the thread returned to its natural flow.

When Lena opened her eyes, she was back in the in-between, the threads of time stretching endlessly around her. She felt a surge of triumph, but also a deep sense of responsibility. This was her role now—not to change time, but to protect it, to ensure its integrity in the face of those who sought to manipulate it.

The Path Forward

As Lena walked through the in-between, she felt a new sense of purpose. She was no longer bound by the limitations of her old life. She had become something more—something timeless. The Talisman pulsed steadily, its hum a reminder that she was never truly alone. Time itself was her ally, her guide.

But Elira's warning lingered in her mind. Others were coming, forces from the far reaches of the universe. Lena knew she couldn't face them alone. She would need to seek allies, to uncover the secrets of the Talisman and the crystal's origins. The universe was vast, and its mysteries were far from fully revealed.

As the threads of time shimmered around her, Lena took a deep breath. She had sealed the crystal, saved the world from immediate collapse. But her journey was far from over. The universe was calling to her, and Lena was ready to answer.

With a final step, she let the threads guide her, the hum of the Talisman merging with the rhythm of time itself. Lena smiled faintly, the weight of her destiny settling on her shoulders. She was no longer just a guardian.

She was also a traveler. A seeker. A protector.

The Path Forward

As Lena walked through the in-between, she felt a new sense of purpose. She was no longer bound by the limitations of her old life. She had become something more—something timeless. The Talisman pulsed steadily, its hum a reminder that she was never truly alone. Time itself was her ally, her guide.

But Elira's warning lingered in her mind. Others were coming, forces from the far reaches of the universe. Lena knew she couldn't face them alone. She would need to seek allies, to uncover the secrets of the Talisman and the crystal's origins. The universe was vast, and its mysteries were far from fully revealed.

A World Reconnected

The rippling threads of time surrounded her, stretching endlessly into the horizon. Each thread represented a moment, a possibility, a choice. Some threads were vibrant, alive with potential, while others were dark and frayed, like fragile remnants of what once was. Lena walked among them, her hand occasionally brushing against the shimmering strands. Each contact brought with it a flicker of memory or insight—a world she might visit, a danger she might face.

The Talisman pulsed again, its rhythm deep and resonant, pulling Lena toward one particular thread. She hesitated, staring at it. The thread vibrated at a frequency that felt almost familiar, yet alien. When she touched it, the sensation was immediate—a rush of sound and light, as though the universe itself was gasping.

Lena stepped forward, allowing herself to merge with the thread's flow. In an instant, she was no longer in the in-between. She stood on the deck of a ship, its sleek design hovering amongst an endless ocean of stars. The air hummed with technology far beyond anything she had encountered before, and the people around her—humanoids with sharp features and glowing eyes—spoke in hushed, urgent tones.

"Temporal distortions are increasing," one of them said, their voice melodic but grave. "If the fractures spread, this entire quadrant will collapse."

Lena felt her chest tighten. She hadn't meant to step into their moment, but her presence seemed unnoticed, as though she were an observer rather than an intruder. She moved through the room, absorbing the details—the advanced technology, the urgency in their voices, the way their eyes flicked toward a central console displaying a holographic map. At its center, pulsing faintly, was an unmistakable symbol: the same markings she had seen on the crystal.

The realization hit her like a tidal wave. The crystal's influence extended far beyond Earth, far beyond anything she had imagined. Its power, its purpose, was part of a larger, universal system—one that spanned galaxies, civilizations, and timelines. And it wasn't just her planet that was at stake.

Lena clenched her fists. This wasn't a random encounter. The Talisman had brought her here for a reason, showing her that the crystal's power was both a gift and a danger on a cosmic scale. She needed to understand more. To protect more.

Before she could act, the Talisman pulsed again, and the vision faded. Lena found herself back in the in-between, the threads of time shifting and flowing around her. Her breath came in shallow gasps, her mind racing with the implications of what she had just seen. The crystal wasn't just a key to time; it was a keystone for the balance of the universe.

The Guardian's Resolve

The Talisman continued to pulse, and Lena knew she couldn't stay in one place for long. The in-between was a refuge, a space for contemplation, but it wasn't a destination. She had a mission now, one that extended beyond what she had initially thought possible.

She walked toward a glowing thread, this one brighter than the rest. It seemed to call to her, vibrating in harmony with the Talisman. As she reached for it, a faint voice echoed in her mind—not Elira's, but something older, deeper.

"Protect the balance. Guard the flow. The Talisman is not yours to keep; it is yours to carry."

The words sent a shiver down her spine, but they also filled her with a strange sense of peace. The Talisman was a tool, a guide, but it wasn't hers to control. She was its steward, its guardian, chosen not for her power, but for her ability to listen, to adapt, to protect without disrupting.

As Lena stepped into the thread, she felt the familiar rush of energy, the sensation of being pulled through the fabric of time. When she emerged, she found herself standing in a vast library, its towering shelves filled with books and scrolls that seemed to hum with their own energy. The air smelled of old parchment and something faintly metallic.

A figure stepped into view—a man with silver hair and piercing eyes. He studied Lena for a moment before speaking. "You're late," he said, his tone amused but not unkind.

"Late for what?" Lena asked, her hand instinctively tightening around the Talisman.

"For your next lesson," he replied, gesturing toward a glowing table in the center of the room. "You've sealed the crystal. You've stabilized the flow of time—for now. But there's more you need to understand. The Talisman has chosen you, but its power is only as strong as your knowledge."

Lena hesitated as the man's calm demeanor put her at ease. She stepped forward, her curiosity outweighing her uncertainty. As she approached the table, she saw that it was inscribed with symbols—markings that mirrored those on the crystal and the Talisman. They pulsed faintly, as if waiting for her to unlock their secrets.

"Who are you?" Lena asked, glancing at the man.

"A guide," he said simply. "Nothing more, nothing less. The universe has many guardians, Lena. You're not the first, and you won't be the last. But your role is unique. The crystal has shown you its potential, and now it's up to you to decide how to use that knowledge."

Lena nodded, the weight of his words settling over her. She reached out, her fingers brushing against the glowing symbols. As she did, a surge of energy flowed through her, filling her with visions of possibilities—worlds she had never imagined, timelines she had never explored, and dangers she had never considered.

The hum of the Talisman deepened, its rhythm merging with the flow of the symbols. Lena closed her eyes, allowing the energy to guide her. She didn't know what the future held, but she knew one thing for certain: her journey was far from over.

An Open Door

When Lena opened her eyes, the library was gone. She stood once more at the edge of the in-between, the threads of time stretching endlessly around her. The Talisman was quiet now, its hum a steady presence against her chest.

She looked out at the threads, her resolve solidifying. The universe had entrusted her with a monumental task, one that spanned far beyond her understanding. But she wasn't afraid. She had learned to navigate the currents of time, to move through its folds without disrupting its flow. And she had the Talisman to guide her.

As she took her first step forward, a faint smile crossed her lips. The path ahead was uncertain, but it was hers to walk. The universe, vast and unpredictable, was waiting.

And Lena was ready.

Chapter 1
In this version, we've kept Lena in Grade 6, with her having the same dream and buzzing connection to the crystal clock, but the setting and context now reflect her age and the school environment. The mysterious note pushes her even further into the mystery of the crystal clock and sets the stage for her journey ahead.

Chapter 2
In this version, the **conflict** centers around Lena's failure to complete her assignment and the humiliation she faces when she admits it in front of the class. Her teacher's disbelief and the subsequent call to her mother add to the **isolation** Lena feels. The chapter concludes with Lena retreating into herself, marking a turning point where she begins to withdraw from her peers and feels misunderstood.

Chapter 3
In this version, Lena attempts to share her dream and the story of the crystal clock with her classmates, but she is met with disbelief and humiliation. Her teacher accuses her of lying and even slaps her in front of the class. The chapter ends with Lena feeling violated, but still resolute in her belief that the crystal clock is real.

Chapter 4
Lena is now a senior in high school, and her quest for knowledge has led her to quantum physics, guided by her new mentor, Mrs. Harrison, the librarian. Through her discussions with Mrs. Harrison, Lena starts to connect the dots between her dreams of the crystal clock and the scientific concepts of quantum entanglement and the theory of relativity. The chapter ends with Lena more determined than ever to uncover the truth about the clock and the power it holds.

Chapter 5
Lena's dreams grow more vivid and detailed, leading her to believe that the crystal clock is part of an ancient system designed to protect time and space. She delves deeper into quantum mechanics, energy frequencies, and the interconnection of the universe, which gives her new insight into the potential power of the clock. Lena now believes the clock is real, and she is being called to find it, though she still has many questions and uncertainties.

Chapter 6
Lena graduates from high school and prepares for the next chapter of her life—attending the University of California to study Cultural Anthropology. Although the ceremony marks a milestone, her heart remains focused on the mysteries of the crystal clock and the energy that has always drawn her toward ancient civilizations. Mrs. Harrison, her librarian and mentor, continues to support her pursuit of knowledge, encouraging her to keep seeking the hidden connections of the universe.

Chapter 7
Lena receives an invitation to join a research team in Peru to investigate the Nazca Lines and high-energy sites in the Andes. On the plane ride there, she experiences a powerful vision of the Crystal Clock, feeling its calling and realizing that it is deeply connected to ancient sites and energy frequencies. The chapter sets the stage for Lena's deeper journey into the Andes, as she believes that the answers she has been searching for are finally within reach.

Chapter 8
Lena and her team discover a towering, 20-foot-high crystal in the hidden temple, and Lena experiences a powerful vision that reveals the crystal's importance. But the moment they uncover its power, danger looms—others are searching for the crystal, and they are willing to fight to take it. The chapter sets the stage for a dangerous confrontation, as Lena realizes that the crystal is not just a key to her dreams, but a force that could change everything.

Chapter 9
Lena's sense of isolation and distrust as she confronts the looming
threat posed by both external forces and internal conflicts within her
team. Tension rises as Lena encounters both allies and enemies, with
the discovery of the crystal triggering a chain of events that leads to
the realization that there are others who seek its power.

Chapter 10
Lena receives much-needed spiritual guidance and is given a sacred
crystal pendant by the Shaman, marking the next step in her journey.
This moment deepens her understanding of her purpose and the vast
responsibility that lies ahead in protecting the Crystal Clock. The story
begins to take on a deeper, more mystical tone, as Lena learns more
about the ancient forces at play.

Chapter 11
In this chapter, Lena uncovers the truth of the Crystal Clock as she
returns to the hidden chamber in the temple. The crystal's power to
manipulate time is revealed, and Lena experiences the moment of
clarity she had been waiting for, as she begins to understand her
connection to the crystal and the potential it holds.

Chapter 12
In this chapter, Lena experiments with the power of the crystal,
manipulating small shifts in time. However, as she realizes the
potential consequences of even minor changes, the weight of her
actions starts to sink in. Her experiment leads to an unexpected
encounter with the professor, who becomes aware of her power, and
the tension begins to build around the risks of altering the fabric of
time.
Chapter 13
In this chapter, Lena is pursued by her rivals, who are determined to
steal the Talisman and the crystal's power. The tension escalates as
Lena narrowly escapes, using the energy from the crystal to open a
hidden passage. But as she evades capture, she realizes that the
professor may not be the ally she thought he was, and that the stakes
of this chase are much higher than she initially understood. The
danger is only beginning.

Chapter 14

In this chapter, Lena learns more about the civilization that created the crystal clock and the dangerous consequences of time manipulation. She begins to understand that she has been chosen as its guardian, meant to protect it from those who would misuse its power. The weight of this responsibility becomes clear, and Lena resolves to safeguard the crystal and its secrets, no matter the cost.

Chapter 15

In this chapter, Lena grapples with the moral dilemma of whether to manipulate time again in order to prevent a catastrophe or to leave the past unchanged. Ultimately, she decides to risk using the crystal's power, understanding that the consequences may be grave but feeling compelled to act in the face of imminent danger. Her decision marks a turning point, and she prepares herself for the challenges that lie ahead.

Chapter 16

In this chapter, Lena embraces her connection to the Crystal Clock, mastering her ability to control time and energy. She faces off against her rivals, who seek to steal the crystal's power for their own purposes, and ultimately uses the crystal's energy to neutralize them. Lena's mastery of the crystal's power marks a turning point in her journey, as she steps fully into her role as the Guardian of Time.

Chapter 17

In this chapter, Lena experiences the destabilizing effects of the crystal's power as reality itself begins to fracture. Time unravels, and Lena is forced to confront the consequences of her actions. Realizing that she may have triggered this collapse, Lena seeks the guidance of the Shaman, hoping he can help her restore balance before it's too late.

Chapter 18

In this chapter, Lena confronts the consequences of her actions, seeking redemption by returning to the crystal cave to undo the damage caused by her manipulation of time. With the guidance of the Shaman's wisdom, Lena makes the ultimate decision to seal the crystal away, hoping to restore balance and prevent further disruption of time's natural flow. However, as she seals the crystal, she is left with a lingering sense of uncertainty—wondering if her actions will truly be enough to protect the world from the unpredictable forces of time.

Chapter 19

In this chapter, Lena reflects on the aftermath of sealing the crystal and the profound changes she has undergone. Although she has saved the world, the questions surrounding her role and the purpose of the crystal linger. With the hum gone and the dreams fading, Lena is left to wonder if she truly understands her place in the universe. As the story closes, she faces a new beginning—one filled with uncertainty, but also with the possibility of discovery.

Chapter 20

In this chapter, Lena is introduced to Elira, a mysterious figure with knowledge of the crystal's deeper implications. Lena learns that there are forces far beyond her understanding searching for the crystal's power. The future of the universe depends on what Lena chooses to do next, setting the stage for a new adventure and the unfolding of an even greater mystery.

The Clock That Stopped Time

Unlock the Power of Generosity With a positive Book Review.

People who give without expecting anything in return live happier lives. So, let's make a difference together!

Would you help someone just like you—curious about The Clock That Stopped Time but unsure where to start?

My mission is to make The Clock That Stopped Time easy and entertaining for everyone.

But to reach more people, I really need your help.

***Most people choose books based on <u>reviews</u>. So, I'm asking you to help a fellow someone interested in Fiction, Fantasy and Mythology by leaving a review.

It costs nothing and takes just a couple of minute but could change someone's view and interest in the journey. Your review could help...

...one more small businesses provide for their community.
...one more entrepreneur support their family.
...one more employee get meaningful work.
..one more client transform their life.
...one more dream come true.

If you love helping others, you're my kind of person. Thank you from the bottom of my heart!

www.ingramcontent.com/pod-product-compliance
Lightning Source LLC
Chambersburg PA
CBHW021527150726
47990CB00006B/2125